TEDDY ONE-EYE

TEDDY ONE-EYE

THE AUTOBIOGRAPHY OF A TEDDY BEAR

GAVIN BISHOP

RANDOM HOUSE
NEW ZEALAND

The assistance of Creative New Zealand is gratefully acknowledged by the publisher.

A RANDOM HOUSE BOOK published by Random House New Zealand
18 Poland Road, Glenfield, Auckland, New Zealand

For more information about our titles go to www.randomhouse.co.nz

A catalogue record for this book is available from the National Library of New Zealand

Random House New Zealand is part of the Random House Group
New York   London   Sydney   Auckland   Delhi   Johannesburg

First published 2014

© 2014 text and illustrations Gavin Bishop

The moral rights of the author have been asserted

ISBN 978 1 77553 727 4
eISBN 978 1 77553 728 1

Design: Carla Sy
Illustrations: Gavin Bishop

Printed in China by RR Donnelly

Some of the passages from *Ruth Fielding and the Gypsies* that appear in this book have been modified from the original.

Every effort has been made by the publisher to contact copyright holders.

To Russell, the best baby
brother anyone could ask for.

CONTENTS

1
OUT OF THE BOX
INVERCARGILL 1950

HE LIFTED ME OUT of the box and hugged me. From that moment on we became best friends. We did everything together. I rode in the back of his trike. I sat next to him at lunch time as he sipped his warm milk. And I lay on the floor in front of the fire and watched him colour in. He showed me how to not go over the edges.

I am not sure where I came from. I remember waking up as a shaft of winter light flooded my box, the box with a logo of four stars and 'Southern Cross Toys — New Zealand' printed on the lid. Was that my birth, my beginning? I'm not sure. In fact, I felt not that I'd been born but as if I had woken from a long sleep. I had the feeling I had been somewhere else, and dreaming, and all memories of that time had blown apart like a cobweb in the wind.

My job now, though, was to be a friend to Boy. He had just been given a new baby brother.

'Your little brother is too small to play with yet,' I heard his grandmother say. 'But you can play with Teddy instead.'

That was me, Mr Edward K. Bear, a new teddy bear. A present from the boy's grandmother. My fur was the colour of sunshine and my eyes were made of shiny brown glass with flecks of gold. They flashed and twinkled when the flames made fiery pictures in the fireplace or when the morning sun came in under the bedroom blind. My perky ears sat straight up on top of my head and listened to everything being said even if it was whispered behind a closed door. And my nose could smell a jar of honey in the kitchen cupboard with the door closed.

The new baby brother, like Boy, had been born in Invercargill, the southernmost city in New Zealand.

'Nothing between here and Antarctica, except Bluff,' Boy's father was fond of saying, shivering as he said so. He came from further up the track in Dunedin, and talked about his hometown as if it were tropical.

But, cold or not, Boy liked Invercargill. He and his mother came down on the train from their home in Kingston to see his grandmother at least twice a year. His dad usually stayed behind. He had a job on the railways, loading and unloading trains that went to and from Invercargill.

Kingston was not much more than a handful of houses, a pub and a school sprinkled along a gravel road at the southern end of Lake Wakatipu. Invercargill was big and exciting. There were shops to visit, playgrounds to have fun in, and a few blocks from where Boy's grandmother lived were the Number Two Gardens with 'the birds'.

2
THE BIRDS

AT THE END OF A CRUNCHY PATH by a hedge of macrocarpa was an aviary, a cage of mismatched birds. Canaries flitted from roost to roost; a guinea fowl took dust baths in the sun; a peacock strutted back and forth displaying its tail feathers; and a kea climbed the netting walls with its beak and claws. This was Boy's favourite place. He took me there as soon as I arrived.

His grandmother hobbled behind as he flew down the

footpath on his trike. 'Be careful,' called the old lady. 'Or you'll be sorry!' I sat in the back tray of the trike and nearly fell out twice — once when the boy swerved to miss a lamp-post, and once when a back wheel slipped into the gutter. 'If you lose that teddy bear you won't get another one like him,' shouted his grandmother.

Boy wanted to 'go to the birds' every day, and most days he did. Even if it was raining his grandmother would follow behind his trike on her arthritic legs, raincoat flapping, calling to him to slow down. I held on tightly in the back. It was fun. It was thrilling in a way I had never felt before: excitement and fear, the perfect mixture for an adventure.

'Mamma spoils you,' Boy's mother would say when we got back to the house.

But soon the holidays were over. It was time to take the new baby home. The boys' dad had gone back to work in Kingston days ago.

'We can't go to the birds today,' said Boy's mother one morning. 'Home today. Train this afternoon.'

'But I want to go to the birds! And I want to go now!'

'There is no time. Play with Teddy while I pack our things.'

But Boy did not listen. He threw me into the back of

his trike and very quietly rode down the path at the side of the house, past the big rhododendron, to the gate. He lifted the latch. And like a rocket on its way to the moon, he took off down the footpath in the direction of the Number Two Gardens.

Yippeeee! Excitement and fear! We were off on another adventure!

But three blocks away he was spotted. Jimmy Cooke from next door was pedalling home from night shift.

'Where are you off to, matey?' asked Jimmy. He blocked the footpath with the front wheel of his bike. Boy had to stop. I looked up from the back tray.

'I'm going to see the birds.'

'Not on your own, are you?'

'Mamma's busy. Mum's packing. Dad's gone home.'

'What about that new baby brother of yours?' asked Jimmy. 'Won't he miss you?'

'Nah, he sleeps all the time. He's not much fun.'

'Give him a chance. He'll grow. But listen, you shouldn't be on your own.'

'I've got Teddy,' said Boy.

'He won't be much help if you get lost.'

I silently shouted that I knew the way to and from the birds as well as anyone, and besides I was enjoying another thrilling ride in the back of the trike.

'Just a minute,' said Jimmy. 'Let's see what I've got left in my lunch tin.'

The birds faded from Boy's mind as his stomach made a hungry gurgle. Jimmy handed him a slice of fudge cake.

'All right,' said Boy, 'I'll go home.'

Holding the cake between his teeth, he turned the handlebars of his trike and slowly pedalled his way back along the footpath towards 121 Ettrick Street where his grandmother and mother were calling for him.

'I've been worried sick,' shouted his mother, grabbing the boy's arm and dragging him off his trike. 'Don't you do that again.'

'Don't be angry with him,' said his grandmother.

'I've got a good mind to give your trike away to Frankie Gibbs! He's not lucky like you are. He'd love a trike like yours.'

'Leave him be,' said his grandmother. 'I'll see to it.'

Boy was bawling. I was still lying in the back of the trike, wondering whether I might be given away or sent back to the toy shop. Was this the end to all the fun we'd been having?

Boy's mother went inside. I heard her stomp into the spare bedroom and start throwing clothes into a suitcase.

This woke the baby, who was sleeping in the same room. He began screaming.

Boy's grandmother said, 'Come with me. I'll make you a piece.'

Still snivelling, Boy picked me out of the back of his trike and followed his grandmother into the kitchen. The old lady cut a slice of bread from the loaf in the bread tin. She grated some cheese onto it and slid it onto a tray in her oven. She switched on the gas and lit it with a match. She poured some milk into a mug with a transfer of a gingerbread man on the side and stirred in two large teaspoons of sugar.

'There, that'll sort you out.'

'Mamma,' sniffed Boy, 'will you read me a story?'

'Aye, by and by, but first I've got something to tell you.'

Boy climbed up onto a stool and propped me up next to him. He picked up his drink with both hands and looked over the top of the mug at his grandmother.

Things had quietened down in the bedroom.

'What do you want to tell me?'

'Well,' said his grandmother, 'around the corner there is a dairy . . .'

'I know that, Mamma, I've been there lots of times.'

'Aye, but at the dairy there is something you should know about.'

Boy took a big slurp of his drink. He put his mug down and looked out of the corner of his eye.

'There is something there you wouldn't like . . .'

'Like what?' The boy turned and faced his grandmother.

'A beast!'

'What sort of beast?' asked Boy.

'A nasty beast with dirty claws and teeth like meat skewers!'

'I've never seen him. And I've been there lots and lots of times!'

'Oh, he's there all right, and if you run away again . . . he will catch you and eat you up!'

'Aw, you're telling fibs!' Boy grabbed me by the head and ran outside.

'Your mousetrap is ready,' called the old lady.

I looked through the back door and saw Boy's mother come into the kitchen, burping the baby on her shoulder.

'Where is he now?'

'Out the back.'

'He's not going to take off again, I hope.'

'I'm pretty sure he won't,' said the old lady as she cut the mousetrap into fingers with her sharpest kitchen knife.

3
THE BEAST

THE TRAIN TO KINGSTON was due to leave at 12.30 that afternoon.

'We seem to be out of milk. I'll pop around to the dairy to get some. I'd like a cuppa before we leave,' said Boy's mother. 'You can come with me,' she said to her son. 'You'll be sitting for a long time on the train.'

'Can I ride my trike?'

'It's been put away in the shed.'

'Can I bring Teddy?'

'All right.'

We set off along the footpath, passed Bubs Wood's place with her five kids, Jimmy Cooke's cottage where he lived with his mother, and Miss Frost's house. As we turned the corner at the end of the street, we almost walked into a painted sign shaped like a hand with a pointing finger. A bit further on, a little brick dairy plastered with advertisements for creaming soda and banana splits stood behind a bed of petunias and a thick concrete curb painted blue.

'Wait by the door. I'll only be a minute,' said Boy's mother.

'I want to come in too.'

'No, you'll only nag for chews. I'm not buying you any today.'

Boy perched on the edge of the curb. He clutched me tightly and absent-mindedly chewed on my right ear.

There was a movement by the door. Boy looked over, expecting to see his mother with a bottle of milk. Instead, a bulldog came bustling out, his tiny eyes squinting in the bright sunlight. He was snorting loudly, and saliva hung in long strings from his wide turned-down mouth. Boy could not believe it. The beast! It was the beast! His grandmother had not been telling fibs. She was right all the time.

A loud scream pierced the morning air. The bulldog raced around the side of the shop and hid behind a stack of milk crates.

Boy's mother came running outside.

'What on earth have you been doing now?'

'The beast! I saw the beast!'

'Time we went back to Kingston. You'll be the death of me,' said Boy's mother. 'That train can't leave soon enough as far as I'm concerned.'

'But I saw the beast. He came out of the dairy.' Boy burst into tears. He dropped me onto the footpath. 'Mamma said that if I ran away again the beast at the dairy would get me . . . and here he is.'

'I can't see any beast,' said his mother.

Boy stopped bellowing and opened his eyes.

'He was just there! When you were in the shop!'

'You and your imagination,' said his mother. 'Come on. Pick Teddy up. The baby will be awake soon.'

Boy hugged me to his chest as we bustled along the street. He whimpered into the back of my neck.

After lunch we got a taxi to the railway station. With a paper bag containing two mutton pies and a cake of milk chocolate for the journey home, we hurried onto the platform. The baby's pram and our suitcases were lifted into the guard's van, and Mrs Hedges from the magazine and cigarette shop rushed over to hold the baby while Boy's mother climbed the steep steps into a carriage.

Boy and I sat beside the window while the train slowly made its way through the outskirts of Invercargill. As it picked up speed, the rhythm of the wheels on the steel tracks fell into a regular beat. Boy grabbed his mother's arm.

'Can you hear it?'

The train was talking to him! It was saying the same thing over and over again: 'the beast, the beast, the beast, the beast . . . here comes the beast, here comes the beast, here comes the beast . . .

'. . . *whooooooOOOOOooooooooooooOOOOooo . . .*'

And when I listened hard, I could hear it too, quite clearly.

4
ROUGH LOVE
KINGSTON 1951

THE BABY BROTHER GREW QUICKLY. By the time
he was 11 months old, he wasn't walking but he could
scoot across a linoleum floor faster than a stone on an icy
pond. He loved squeezing the cat's neck or pulling its tail
and, if Boy left me within reach, BB pulled me onto the
floor and wrestled with me. When he was teething, my
paws seemed to offer him comfort, so he chewed them.

As his teeth broke through his gums, their little rough edges tore at the tender fabric on the ends of my arms and legs. Boy didn't like this. He would snatch me from his little brother and hide me carefully in another part of the house.

Most of the time, Boy was good to me. He tucked me up in bed with him at night and brushed my coat. If he ever forgot to be gentle, and swung me around by one arm or jumped on me, it was because we were having fun. We had lots of fun. I laughed and laughed (silently), and was always ready for one of his adventures.

These took place outside, usually in the wheelbarrow, which in Kingston replaced the trike. The wheelbarrow was even more thrilling than the trike. There were wobbly rides across the rough paddocks behind the house or over the bumpy gravel at the sides of the railway tracks. Black Nin, the dog from the pub, would sometimes run along beside us, barking. This added to the excitement. But I was growing to dislike this dog. If Boy was not careful, Black Nin would snatch me from the barrow and run off to a quiet place behind a broom bush or a clump of foxgloves and gnaw on me as if I were a beef bone. When I was finally rescued, my coat was dripping with dog slobber. It was more excitement and fear though, all part of an adventure with Boy.

I usually had the wheelbarrow to myself, but sometimes I had to share it. A heavy tin tractor with knobbly
tyres, a nervous cat with sharp claws, or a pile of dirt
dug from the vegetable garden was often thrown in with
me. The cat didn't last long. It jumped out as soon as the
wheelbarrow journey began. But the truck liked to roll
backwards and forwards and bump into me. And the dirt
moved and shifted until I was half-buried, with only my
nose and one eye poking out.

At bedtime I was dragged from the dirt and given a
quick brush. Boy liked to feel me lying beside him in bed.
He would tuck one of my arms under his neck and put one
of my big glass eyes between his teeth as if it were a lolly.
Every night he did this. But by morning, because the boy
tossed and turned, dreaming, I suspected, of the beast at
the dairy, I was usually on the floor or sitting in the box of
comics that Boy kept beside his bed.

Now there was no fear of being returned to the toy
shop or given away if Boy misbehaved. After almost a year,
my golden coat was bedraggled, my paws were chewed
and my eyes were loose. I was no longer a new bear.

5
THE FIRST PATCHES

AT THE END OF THE WINTER when frosts were less likely, Boy's grandmother came to stay. She slept in the spare bedroom off the kitchen, in a single bed next to the Singer sewing machine. Its folded-down top was just big enough to take her knitting bag, a book, her reading glasses and a tumbler to soak her teeth in. The room was wallpapered with a pattern of tiny pink daisies that she said reminded her of a garden she once knew as a girl, when she lived in

Riverton. The heat from the coal range kept her room warm, if she remembered to keep the door open.

In the small brown suitcase slipped under the bed, she had neatly packed two woollen dresses, a pair of black shoes with a sensible heel, and her slippers. There were three floral aprons edged with rickrack made by one of her daughters as a Christmas present. She wore one of these every day to keep her clothes clean and to show she was ready to roll out a batch of scones, slice up some beetroot or pluck a chook. And there were fine woollen singlets from the mills in Mosgiel, which she tucked down well into her bloomers. The bloomers were designed to reach her knees and cover the gap at the top of her lisle stockings that were, by far, her most important items of clothing. 'A woman is not properly dressed until she has covered her legs,' she would say. She always travelled with two pairs of stockings. One pair still in its packet — a pair for best; and the other pair, for second-best, to be worn every day, summer or winter, hot or cold, wet or fine. Her lisle stockings were thick and brown. 'Bullet-proof!' was the way Boy's father described them.

And underneath all of these items in her suitcase were her button tin and a mending kit with a range of different-sized needles and reels of cotton in a variety of colours.

She went nowhere without the kit and the tin.

She liked reading stories to Boy. But when she tried to sing one of her old songs or recite a rhyme to BB, she didn't get very far. He would not sit still long enough. Down off her knee he would slide to crawl across the floor and grab a handful of the cat's fur or play in the coal bucket.

She seemed happy to be in Kingston once again with Boy and his family, until she saw my torn paws and dirty fur. 'What's up with Teddy?' she cried. 'He's in a terrible state! He's only a few months old.'

'Actually,' said Boy, 'he's nearly a year old. He is the same age as my baby brother. And he is almost . . . one . . . year . . .'

Boy's grandmother gave him one of her looks. She stabbed her knitting needles into a ball of wool and picked me up off the floor. She rose from the couch, carried me into her bedroom and firmly closed the door. From the mending kit in her suitcase, she picked out a needle and threaded it from a reel of brown cotton. She sat on the bed with me across her lap, and set to work mending the tears and rips in my feet and paws.

After a while she stopped. 'This is no good,' she said. 'The holes are too big.'

She stood up and opened the door.

'Do you have any material I can use?' she called to the boys' mother.

'What colour do you want?'

'Brown!' grunted the old woman. 'How did you let those boys do this to their teddy bear?'

'I don't have eyes in the back of my head, Mum.'

'This bear is special. You won't get another one like him!'

'Look,' said the boys' mother, 'I've got two kids to look after, a house to keep and a cow to milk. What more do you want me to do?'

Both of the women suddenly went quiet. The two boys were watching them. I peeked up from the old lady's bed where she had left me.

'I didn't do anything to Teddy,' said Boy. 'It was his fault.' He gave his little brother a shove. BB started to cry.

His mother picked him up and said over her shoulder, 'Have a look in the basket under the sewing machine. You might find some material there you can use.'

Boy's grandmother spent the next hour patching my paws and feet with some fawn fabric that had been used to make a pair of Boy's overalls. When she had finished, she came out of the bedroom and gave me back to Boy.

'Now look after him,' she said. 'Or I'll tell the pixies to take him off to fairyland.'

6
READING LESSONS

A FEW NIGHTS LATER, after tea, when pyjamas were on and teeth were brushed, it was time for a story. BB was already asleep.

'I would like a different story tonight please, Mamma,' said Boy. The old lady looked up. She was crocheting around the edge of a pillowcase.

'I've heard all my books over and over again. I want a different book.'

'Well, I haven't got anything that you would like.'

Boy turned to his mother. 'Mum, do you have any more books?'

'I don't think so.' She paused from putting the dishes away. 'But I'll have a look.'

A few minutes later she came back with an old book with a dark-green cover.

'I got this when I was dux of Mossburn Primary School,' she said in a way that demanded a response.

Boy took the book and opened the thick, soft pages. It had a dry, musty smell like a dusty cupboard full of secrets. He tried to read the title.

'Ruu . . . th . . .' he said.

'*Ruth Fielding and the Gypsies*,' read his mother. 'By Alice B. Emerson. It's a girl's book. I mean . . . it's about a girl, but I think you'll find it exciting.'

'It smells exciting,' said Boy, who wasn't used to books as thick or as grown-up-looking as this one.

Boy's grandmother took the book and opened it at the first page. 'It's quite long,' she said. 'We'll have a chapter a night.'

Boy tucked me under his arm and climbed onto the sofa beside his grandmother. 'Mind my crochet,' she said. He nestled into her, and when he had stopped squirming she opened the book, turned over the first few pages and started to read.

'*Chapter One, On the Lumanu River.*

'*The steady turning of the grinding-stones set the old Red Mill a-quiver in every board and beam. The air within was full of dust — dust of the grain, and fine, fine dust from the stones themselves.*'

'Are you sure you are going to like this?' The old lady put her finger between the pages and closed the book.

'Yes! It's really good!' said Boy.

I was enjoying it too, even though I wasn't sure what *grinding stones* were. I was wondering, though, when the story was going to start.

Boy's grandmother turned back to the book and continued to read. Soon we were introduced to Ruth Fielding, the main character. She lived at Red Mill with her Aunt Alvirah and Uncle Jabez, who was a miller.

'*Now, Ruth Fielding was worth looking at. She was plump, but not too plump. In her tanned cheeks the blood flowed richly. Her cheeks were perhaps a little too round; her nose — well, it was not a dignified nose at all!*'

Boy began to squirm. I would have too, if I hadn't been tucked so tightly into the gap between him and the sofa. The story wasn't very interesting. But I watched the words as the old lady read to us. I saw that the sounds were echoed in the shapes on the page. I was learning to read.

'Do you want me to go on?' asked Boy's grandmother.

'Yeah . . . it's good.'

'Sure?'

'Yep.'

Next we heard how Ben, the hired hand, was away and could not deliver three bags of flour to the baker across the river. Ruth said she could help. So she and her uncle loaded the bags of flour into the old rowboat.

Things were looking up. The story was getting more exciting. Boy was sitting quietly, listening.

Ruth and her uncle rowed out onto the river. Quite quickly, the currents grew stronger and the rowboat was swept too far downstream.

Now, Boy was staring off into a faraway place. I was holding my breath while I listened and watched the words.

Suddenly the boat whirled around and struck a rock. The rotting planks of the rowboat caved in. The old boat tipped and Uncle Jabez fell into the water.

'*Blood-stained bubbles rose to the surface, and the old man struggled to rise out of the water.*

'*Although she was a good swimmer, it was doubtful if Ruth Fielding could save both the miller and herself from the peril that menaced them.*'

'Time for bed,' said Boy's grandmother.

'But it's just getting really exciting!'

'That's the end of the chapter. A chapter a night is what I said.'

I wanted her to go on reading too. I wanted to know if Ruth Fielding would be able to save her uncle from drowning. But when the old lady said something, she meant it.

She placed three long pieces of red wool from her knitting bag between the pages of the book. The place was marked. The book would wait for us to come visiting the following night.

Boy quickly fell asleep. He didn't have time to put my arm in the usual place nor put one of my eyes between his teeth. But his sleep was fitful. He threw his arms above his head. His sheets became tangled around his legs. It was a relief to be tossed out onto the cold lino floor and escape the heat of his dreams.

I lay thinking about Ruth Fielding. She was kind and brave. She reminded me of someone I thought I once knew, before I came to live with the boy. Someone else called Ruth. But how could that be? My life started when the box was opened in Invercargill just after BB was born. Or did it?

7
AFTERNOON STORIES

'DID YOU HAVE A NICE BIG SLEEP?' asked Boy's dad next morning. 'I had to cover you up when I got home from work last night.'

Boy yawned and stretched. 'I dreamed that you and I were out on the lake in an old boat and it was going to sink.'

'It's that jolly book Mamma was reading you last night,' said his mother. 'You won't be reading any more of it.'

'Oh no, please, it's really good! Teddy likes it too.'

'It's no good if it's going to disturb your sleep.'

Boy's grandmother was spreading some marmalade on a slice of toast.

'Perhaps we should read some when you get home from school while it's still light,' she said.

'Oh, Mum, you spoil that boy,' said Boy's mother.

'Well, it will give the story time to settle before he goes to bed. Besides, I'm keen to find out what will happen next. And I bet Teddy is too.' She cast a glance in my direction.

She was right. I was looking forward to the next chapter. *Ruth Fielding and the Gypsies* was certainly an adventurous book full of excitement and fear. And I wanted to look at some more words while I listened to the sounds they made.

The sun was still high above the house when Boy raced into the kitchen after school. He threw his school bag onto the floor. His mother was cutting up apples for a pie at the kitchen bench.

'Hang your bag up. And be quiet. Your brother is asleep and Mamma's listening to something on the radio.'

At this time of the afternoon his grandmother was usually having a nap. She could sleep through an atomic blast, Boy's dad liked to remind everyone. But today she was sitting on the sofa, awake.

'Twenty-two thousand men are off work,' said the radio news report, 'as disputes on the wharves in Auckland and Wellington go into their second week.'

'I feel for the mothers and the children,' the old lady said. 'Who's going to put food on their tables?'

Tucked under the cushion by her elbow was the book.

'Have you already read some?' asked the boy, ignoring the radio. A row of sweat beads sat on his top lip. 'I ran all the way home. Nearly got caught in some matagouri by the dry creek.'

The old lady brushed his hair from his forehead. 'Go and get yourself a piece and something to drink,' she said.

Boy scooped me up from the toy box. With the other hand he got a pikelet from the cupboard above the sink. He scrambled onto the sofa beside his grandmother and propped me up beside him.

'Don't you want something on your piece?'

Boy usually had marmite and raspberry jam, together — his favourite.

'No thanks, I want to hear the story.'

The old lady turned the radio off and pulled the book out from under the cushion. She opened the pages she had marked with red wool the night before.

'*Chapter Two: Roberto the Gypsy.*'

The chapter started quietly enough. We heard how Ruth Fielding's parents had died when she was a little girl and how she went to live with her mother's uncle at Red Mill. Ruth and her friends were on holiday before beginning a new term at their school called Briarwood Hall.

All the time I was listening, I was watching the words very closely.

'When is the good bit going to start again?' asked Boy.

I was beginning to wonder too.

'Here it is,' said his grandmother, who was just as keen as we were to get on with the adventurous part of the story.

'The hurrying water tugged at her. Her uncle's body was so heavy that she had all she could do to hold his head above the surface.'

The rowboat was sinking, the flour was getting wet and heavy. Ruth started screaming for help but there was no one at the landing. No one could hear her. Her uncle was still unconscious.

Then suddenly she heard . . .

'*"Hold on! I'm coming!"*'

The person came into sight.

'*He was a wild-looking person. His feet were bare and to Ruth he seemed very bronzed and rough looking. His long hair was tangled like a wild man's. In his ears Ruth saw small gold rings and his forearms were covered with an intricate pattern of tattooing in red and blue ink.'*

The strange boy helped Ruth to get her uncle ashore. He introduced himself as Roberto. Then he jumped up and, without a word, fled back into the woods.

Without the slightest pause, the old lady began to read the next chapter. I think she was enjoying the story as much as we were. Boy looked up at her briefly but she took no notice. He didn't say a word.

'That story seems to be taking a long time,' said his mother from the kitchen. 'Did you bring a reading book home from school?'

The reply from the sofa was a silent one.

Chapter Three: Evening at the Red Mill had us both squirming with boredom. There was a lot of discussion about whether girls could do the work of men and whether they should if they could, or whether they shouldn't if they couldn't. There were no exciting river adventures or mysterious gypsy boys.

There was no need to let this chapter settle before going to bed. Nothing had happened to give Boy bad dreams. And as it ended, BB woke up, ready for something to eat. Time for stories was over.

After tea, Boy took the school reading book from his

bag. I looked over his shoulder as he read aloud. We both practised our reading:

'Look, Janet.

Look at the basket.

One kitten runs to the basket.

Jump in, kitten.

Jump in and play.'

Spelling was next:

'. . . date hate plate, bee free queen, fine shine pine . . .'

The boys' mother spread their pyjamas to warm on the rack above the coal range, and Boy nuggeted his boots for the next day. Then it was time for bed.

8
RETURN OF THE BEAST

WE CLIMBED INTO BED. Boy tucked one of my arms beneath his neck and placed one of my eyes between his teeth. After a couple of deep, sleepy breaths, he was asleep. His breathing became heavy and his legs kept moving under the bedclothes as if he were trying to run or perhaps pedal. He was obviously dreaming. And I could tell, somehow, he was dreaming of the dairy in Invercargill. He needed my help.

I started to count backwards from ten. Ten, nine, eight, seven, six . . . five . . . and I slipped smoothly into his dream.

From the back of the trike, I looked up past Boy's left leg and watched as the hokey-pokey ice cream slid over his tongue. I could hear the crunch of the cone as he bit into it. But, I could sense we weren't alone. There was someone behind us. Boy felt it too. He stopped licking and turned. We both saw him at the same time . . . the beast!

He was right behind us. But why was he there? Boy hadn't run away from home. He was allowed to go to the dairy on his own now. He would be six this year and he had his own pocket money. I was even more afraid than Boy. I liked having adventures but I didn't like this one. If the beast attacked me, he would tear me to shreds. Boy's grandmother would never be able to mend me again. Boy knew this too.

Like a soldier going into battle, he slid off the seat of his trike and charged towards the beast, his ice cream thrust out in front of him. He ran straight at the beast and poked his hokey-pokey ice cream into the beast's snubby nose. The dog yelped in surprise. The ice cream slid off his face and the greedy animal lost no time in slurping it up off the footpath. Boy jumped back onto his trike and, with his teeth firmly clenched, he took off down the street.

Meanwhile, back in his bed in Kingston, Boy bit down on my eye — snap! My eye came off. Boy swallowed. My eye went down his throat. He woke up. The beast had gone. He was in his own bed with his best friend, his teddy bear. His teddy bear with one eye missing.

Boy called to his mother. She came running in from the kitchen.

'What is the matter now?' she cried. 'Can't I get any peace?'

'I've swallowed Teddy's eye.'

Boy's mother started to laugh. 'Whatever next?'

She went back out to the kitchen. Boy grabbed me by one arm and followed her.

'I swallowed Teddy's eye.' He looked at his father who had just arrived home after working late, and then at his grandmother.

'I swallowed Teddy's eye!'

His grandmother put her teacup down onto the saucer.

'Then you'll probably die,' she said, turning away to hide her smile.

'Maybe,' said Boy. 'But I'm not scared of that beast anymore.'

'And anyway, old Teddy One-eye will look after you,' said Boy's dad.

'Teddy One-eye! Hey, that's a good name!' Boy beamed.

'Teddy One-eye indeed!' The tiny smile slid from the face of Boy's grandmother. She grabbed her walking stick and stood up. As she reached her bedroom door she turned and said very slowly and sharply: 'Treat that bear with respect. He is very special and you'll never get another one like him!'

9
THE POT CUPBOARD
1952

ON THE LONG DAYS when Boy was at school, I spent my time waiting for him to come home. Both of my arms had been pulled off during fights with his baby brother. BB wanted me for himself, but Boy reminded him that I was his.

So there was always a job for the boys' grandmother when she came for a holiday from Invercargill. She looked very cross as she stitched my arms back on with grey wool, but said nothing except to mutter, 'Boys will be boys, I suppose.'

She had replaced my missing eye with a button from her button tin. And when she held me at arm's length to have a good look at me, she sighed. 'Well, they won't be able to call you Teddy One-eye now.'

But even with two eyes, the new name stuck fast.

The new eye was smaller and I couldn't see as well with it, but I could still read. Yes, I could read . . . perhaps not very well, but I was getting better. I kept it a secret, though. And my hearing was still sharp, even if my ears were squashed.

When Boy left the house, he hid me where BB would not find me. The baby brother could wriggle under beds and climb up to high cupboards, so hiding places had to be carefully planned. One of the best places was the pot cupboard under the sink in the scullery. BB could not open the door to this cupboard because his dad had put a padlock on it to make it baby-proof. His big brother knew the key was in the cutlery drawer.

I spent five days a week hidden behind the big black enamel pot that the corned beef and the muttonbirds were cooked in. I could hear Boy's mother doing dishes or rolling out pastry for a pie above my head. The cat would sometimes sniff at the door of my hideout. I would hold my breath until she went away. I was afraid she would show the baby brother where I was hiding.

On fine days, the crackle of gravel outside the back door meant BB was riding on his little tractor. I could relax. He had forgotten about me. During BB's naptimes I heard the radio playing in the kitchen. Some mornings, Aunt Daisy had a recipe for Cornflour Blancmange or Beetroot Chutney. A radio serial from Australia set in a hospital played at two o'clock each Tuesday. And at other times the boys' mother sang along to songs she liked. One afternoon a special broadcast announced that Yvette Williams had become New Zealand's first female Olympic medallist.

At half-past three Boy came bursting through the back door, looking for something to eat. After wolfing a piece of bread with jam and marmite and gulping down a glass of cordial, he remembered me. He unlocked the cupboard door and pulled me out into the light. I peered about the house with my one-and-a-half eyes to see if anything had changed during my hours in the pot cupboard. And often there were changes. Tiny ones. A vase of daffodils sat in the middle of the dining table. A freshly ironed shirt hung on the back of a chair. A slab of Louise cake sat cooling.

Then it was fun time. Time for adventure. Excitement and fear. 'Let's go, Teddy One-eye!' Boy would throw me into the wheelbarrow and off we would go, through the back gate by the big lilac tree and across the rough paddock to the Greek family's house. Boy always had something for Maritsa the pig — an apple, an old crust of bread or a dry scone. We didn't stay long. Once the pig was fed and we had said hello to the Kariannis kids, we were off again, across another paddock to see Frankie Gibbs.

Next to me, Frankie was Boy's best friend.

Sometimes when we pulled up to the bottom of the steps of Mum O'Donnell's house where Frankie lived, Mum O would poke her head out the door to say that Frankie was not there. He had gone down to Invercargill to see his mum. At times we almost forgot he was a foster kid and Mum O'Donnell's was not his real home. By the time Boy had turned his wheelbarrow around, his mother would be calling us back home.

'Coooeeeee!' Her voice bounced off the Kariannis's pig sty and shot across the long-grass paddocks. 'Tea time!'

The two boys were sat down with a plate of mince, a slice of bread and butter, and a glass of milk before their mother slipped out the back door to go and milk the cow. If they were good, she told them, and didn't fight, there would be some pudding when she got back.

Propped up on the sofa, I would watch the boys with my big glass eye to see which one of them would come to grab me first. With my small button eye I would look out the window, watching for the return of their mother.

While she was away, there were usually fights. Boy would start by whacking me over BB's head. It didn't hurt him — I was pretty soft — but it made him mad. The younger boy would try to wrestle me from his big brother. The fighting continued until the boys' mother came through the back door with a bucket of warm milk.

The boys would fall silent as she looked around the room.

'I hope you two have been good?'

'Yes, Mum!'

Then she would notice me on the floor behind the couch, my ears, legs and even my head torn and ripped.

As she picked me up, shaking her head, she'd say, 'I do wish you boys would stop fighting!'

Once BB was in bed and Boy was busy with a drawing at the kitchen table, she would take a needle and some wool from her sewing basket and do a patch-up job on me.

'Well, Ted,' she'd say, 'this is not as good as Mamma would do, but I think it will last until she comes back.'

If the boys' father got home from work early enough,

it was his job to read the bedtime stories. I always made sure that I was propped up somewhere so I could see the words in the books Boy brought home from school. His dad had decided that *Ruth Fielding and the Gypsies* should be kept and read like a radio serial when Mamma came up from Invercargill.

10
A NIGHT ON THE BEACH
1952

BOY WAS GROWING UP. I noticed he was becoming more interested in playing with Frankie Gibbs or Len Hume than with me. He didn't bother to hide me in the pot cupboard anymore. And he didn't care when I ended up in his baby brother's bed instead of his. In fact, BB now took me everywhere with him. I was his friend when he sat on his potty. I was his cushion when he had his morning snack. And I caught the drips from the watering can as he stood watering the broad beans in his dad's garden. But BB was not as much fun as Boy. He was still too little to take me on adventures.

Then one autumn afternoon that all changed.

'Come on, we'll go and collect some driftwood for the front-room fire,' said BB's mother.

BB jumped up and pushed his tip-truck away across the floor. He ran to pick me up from the couch.

'I think you should leave Teddy One-eye, I mean Teddy, at home,' said BB's mum.

'No!' he screamed, hugging me tightly with both arms.

'All right,' sighed his mother, 'but if you lose him you'll be sorry. You won't get another teddy bear.'

We set off down the gravel path at the side of the house, out the gate, across the railway lines, and through the lupins with bulging seed-heads to the stony beach at the edge of the lake. It looked as if I was going on my first adventure with BB whether he was ready or not. I was nervous but quietly excited.

The little boy slipped and slid in the loose stones, trying to keep up with his mother while she picked up small logs and branches and put them into a sugar bag. I hung from his hand by one arm; my feet dragged along the gravel.

BB soon got tired and sat down. He let go of my paw,

and I fell behind a clump of lupin. My glass eye looked out across the lake and my button eye watched BB.

'I don't want to go any further,' he yelled.

His mother turned back. Her sack was full. She made no comment but sighed as she slung it over her shoulder and hoisted BB onto her hip. He nestled into her neck and slipped his thumb into his mouth. BB's mum slowly trudged back up the stony bank through the lupins and across the railway lines towards the house. My button eye watched them go.

This was not what I had in mind when I hoped to go on an adventure with BB. There was more fear than excitement. I was alone. It was late afternoon. Boy would be home from school soon, but would he notice I was missing? He probably wouldn't, because he didn't play with me anymore. Perhaps no one would notice I was missing until bedtime. And then it would be dark.

In a nearby willow, a bird was singing as if it were trying to catch a tune it had heard somewhere before. Then it stopped.

A seagull landed on a log near my head. It blocked my view of the lake. The bird hopped over and looked down at me. It pecked my nose, once. And then it did it again — twice, three times, four times — until my nose came off. Another seagull landed nearby and screamed. The bird with my nose flew off over the lake. I could see it flying further and further until it dropped something into the water. My nose. It dropped my nose into the deep, cold waters of Lake Wakatipu.

A breeze blew some dead willow leaves along the beach. They built up against me, covering me like a yellow eiderdown, until only my face and one arm could be seen.

The sun went down and a cold wind blew off the lake. The leaves kept me warm. I peered through the gathering darkness, hoping I might see someone coming to look for me.

Then I saw it — a light swinging backwards and forwards. Thank goodness, someone was coming along the beach. They got closer until they were just on the other side of the lupins.

'Here I am! Here I am!' I shouted silently.

But the lamp went past. The scrunch of boots on the gravel got further and further away until I could no longer hear it.

The moon sailed out from behind the clouds above the Hector mountains. It cast a creamy glow over the houses of Kingston. With my button eye I could see the blurry outline of Piano Rock. As I was wondering why Boy and his friends were afraid of that place, a morepork landed on the log where the seagull had stood. It strutted, and flexed its wings, flicking its head from side to side. With one eye at a time it looked into my glass eye with its flecks of gold. Then it swooped and tore a long gash in my arm with its beak before flying off. I can't have been tasty enough.

My next visitor was a slug, slithering across the damp stones from a nearby flax bush. It climbed up my face and, with its skirt rippling along the hem, delicately slipped across my glass eye before making its slimy way down the arm that the morepork had slashed. It paused and inspected the damage, little antennae swaying this way and that, as if it were considering how it might mend the gash, but it moved on and disappeared among the dry leaves.

The lake rose and sighed, gently moving the stones at its edge. A shooting star looked at itself in my shiny eye and the Southern Cross hung like a coronet above my head. I felt comforted by this crown of stars, as if it were floating up there just for me, perhaps promising I would be found and taken safely back home. And then I remembered the stars were the same as those on the box from Southern Cross Toys. The box I had come in as a new teddy bear for Boy. So much had happened to me since that time. I certainly didn't look like the same bear.

The morning light took me by surprise as the sun's fingers stretched across the lake and tapped on my glass eye. Then with my button eye I watched as the sun lightly touched the house by the lagoon and, a little later, the houses across the railway line. Finally, as it reached Piano Rock, I heard the sound of someone calling and running across the stones of the beach.

My answer was silent, but I called back at the top of my voice, 'I'm over here, I'm over here!!!'

As if he had heard me, Boy came to where I was lying in my yellow bed behind the clump of lupins. He picked me up, brushed away the leaves that clung to my fur and gently carried me home.

'Teddy One-eye!' shouted BB. 'You found him!'

'Yes, and *you* are *not* having him.'

His baby brother bawled while Boy stuffed me into his school bag with his lunch tin and his reading book. 'He's coming to school with me.' It was as if Boy suddenly remembered I belonged to him after all.

BB bawled even harder. The house was filled with his caterwauling.

'See you after work,' called his father. He grabbed his own lunch tin and hurried out the back door.

'And I'm going to see to the washing,' said his mother, jumping up from the breakfast table. 'Do you want to come?'

BB stopped crying and followed his mother out to the washhouse.

'Where's the cat?' he asked between sobs.

Boy, with me in his school bag on his back, had already slipped through the back gate to run across the paddock to pick up Frankie Gibbs on the way to school.

It was good to be back with the family again.

11
A YEAR TO REMEMBER
1953

THE SHORT, DARK DAYS in the middle of the year were made brighter one morning by some good news on the radio. Edmund Hillary and Sherpa Tenzing had conquered Mt Everest, the highest mountain in the world. Over the next few weeks, I watched as Boy made a scrapbook of the great event from pictures in the *New Zealand Weekly News*. His dad drew a picture for the cover. Boy did lots of drawings for the book too. He was good at drawing and he wanted to be an artist when he grew up.

Boy's mother was making a scrapbook as well. Not of the Everest conquest, but of the coronation of the new Queen of England. She was leaving plenty of room at the back of her book, because the young Queen and her husband were coming to New Zealand on a visit at the end of the year. Even though the Queen was not visiting Kingston, Boy's mother was determined to see her if it was the last thing she did. Everyone in Kingston seemed to be excited. In fact, if Aunt Daisy was to be believed, everyone in New Zealand could not wait to see the new Queen. Vic Gherkin was having the pub painted, and the kids were planning a special red, white and blue flowerbed at the school. Mr Hume bought a picture of the young Queen for their little cottage up by the main road, even though Mrs Hume thought it was a waste of money.

One Saturday afternoon in spring, Boy's grandmother arrived on the bus from Invercargill. The family had exciting plans. First there would be Guy Fawkes night and then, not too many weeks later, Christmas. A few days after that they would all (though not the dad) go back to Invercargill with their grandmother to see the Queen and her husband, the Duke, before they left at the end of their New Zealand tour.

No sooner had the old lady walked into the kitchen and put down her suitcase than Boy presented her with *Ruth Fielding and the Gypsies.*

'Can you read us some please, Mamma?'

'Let your grandmother take her coat off. And she needs a cup of tea,' said his mother. 'Besides, you are old enough to read that book yourself.'

And so am I, I thought quietly.

'It's not the same,' said Boy.

'I'll be with you directly,' said the old lady. She went into the bedroom off the kitchen and hung her coat on the back of the door. She came back into the room and sat on the sofa.

'Now, where were we?'

'You've still got your hat on,' said BB.

'Ladies can wear their hats inside,' said Boy. 'Be quiet. Let's get started.'

We crowded around the old lady as she opened the book where the red wool marked the place. Boy was on one side, and I sat on BB's knee on the other side. BB liked stories now he was older. And he liked the look of this book because it was fatter than any book he had ever seen.

'*Chapter Four: The Auto Tour.*'

'What's an auto?' asked a small voice from behind my right ear.

'A car! Now be quiet. I want to hear the story,' said Boy.

Ruth and the Cameron twins, Helen and Tom, set off on a trip to see some friends, the Larkins, and to stay a night with the twins' Uncle Ike. Tom was driving an old car that his father had lent him. On the road they rescued Roberto the gypsy boy from the clutches of an angry farmer who was annoyed that Roberto had slept in his barn without paying.

'*Chapter Five: A Prophecy Fulfilled.*'

The old lady began reading the next chapter without a pause.

Roberto travelled with Ruth and her friends until he decided to go on to the gypsy camp by foot. Then Tom became tired of driving slowly.

'*"It's great to go fast!" he exclaimed. "Here's a straight piece of road ahead, girls. Hold on!"*'

'*The girls clung to the hand-holds and Tom crouched behind the windshield and "let her out."*'

Suddenly there was an accident. A lamb had wandered onto the road.

'*"Oh the lamb!" shrieked Helen. The car struck it, and with a pitiful "baa-a-a!" it was knocked off its feet.*'

'*Chapter Six: A Transaction in Mutton.*'

The lamb had a broken leg. Tom paid the angry farmer and they took the lamb with them to Littletop. There they delivered it safely into the hands of Fred Larkin and his family.

The next day, as they continued their journey to Uncle Ike's place, they saw two gypsy men watching them from the side of the road. They went a little further before . . .

'*On a rising stretch of road, the engine began to miss, and something rattled painfully in the "internal arrangements" of the car.*'

Thunderclouds hung over the mountains. The friends spied an old house. The car limped up to the sagging gate but, to their despair, the house was abandoned. It looked gaunt and ghostly!

'Oh, you're not going to stop now,' cried Boy as his grandmother placed the strips of red wool between the pages and closed the book.

'It'll keep,' said the old lady.

'But it's getting really exciting . . .'

'I wish we had a car,' said BB. 'I would drive it all over the hills. I would toot the horn and frighten all the sheep!'

'Don't get carried away,' said his big brother as he slipped off the couch and went off to find some crayons and his drawing pad.

12
A SUNDAY DRIVE

NEXT MORNING BOY ARRIVED home from Sunday school just in time to help his grandmother shell some peas for their midday dinner. His mother was turning the potatoes stacked around the roasting leg of mutton when his father came through the back door.

'Grab your hats, everyone. We're going out!'

'But I'm just about to make the gravy,' said the boy's mother.

'No time for that,' he said.

'The boys need their meal,' said the grandmother. 'What's so urgent that we can't have our dinner first?'

'Vic Gherkin has lent us his car for the afternoon. He says we should go for a spin, blow away the cobwebs. And give his old Ford a run. He says he's too busy behind the bar at the pub to take it out much these days.'

'Can I drive?' asked BB.

'Have you got a licence?' asked his father.

The little boy shook his head.

'I'll get dinner on the table,' said the boys' mother. 'The sooner we have it, the sooner we can go.'

The family wolfed down the roast mutton, potatoes, pumpkin and peas as if they had been cast adrift on an ice floe for three weeks without food.

'Who would like some apple crumble?'

'No thanks, Mum. No time!' said Boy. 'Let's go!'

The leftover meat and vegetables were put in the safe. The fire was dampered. The dishes were rinsed and stacked in the sink.

'Ready!' shouted BB, although he had done nothing to help.

Their grandmother was already on the front lawn with her hat and coat on. She was wearing her best pair of lisle stockings and steadying herself with her walking stick.

'It's in case we feel like an ice cream later,' she said when she saw the boys' mother looking at the big black patent-leather handbag hanging from her arm.

The old car was where the boys' dad had parked it after driving it back from the pub. We piled in. The parents sat in the front. The grandmother, the two boys and I sat in the back. The leather seats were very comfortable and there was even a rug to throw over the grandmother's knees.

The car started first time. Vic Gherkin had said it might have to be cranked, but it coughed into life with only one pull on the ignition. The boys' dad put the car into gear, and as it rolled off along the gravel a little squeaky song could be heard over the hum of the engine, as if the old car were singing a song of the road.

We drove up through Kingston, past the school to the main road.

'Left or right?' asked Dad over his shoulder.

'Right! Turn right!' cried Boy. 'The other way goes over the Devil's Staircase!'

'All right, all right,' said Dad. 'Keep your hair on! I thought we might go to Queenstown. But we can check out Lumsden instead, if you like.'

He turned right at the Humes's place.

In the back seat, the old lady handed Boy a ten-shilling note.

'Hold on to that. You can be the man in the car. When we stop, you can pay for the ice creams.'

Even though the road was dusty and winding, the old lady fell asleep. The boys didn't notice. They were busy playing 'black dog, white horse'. I couldn't see out the window very well because I was squashed between BB and his grandmother. Most of me was under the rug.

The sky above the road was what some people called powder blue. A rough white cloud, like the scribble of a two-year-old, sat just above the hills. It was a perfect day for blowing away the cobwebs, even if there wasn't much of a breeze. The boys' father wound down his window and stuck his elbow out. He started to sing 'Beautiful Dreamer' as a duet with the car's squeaky song.

He had just reached the end of the first verse when the car gave a lurch. Dad pulled the car to a stop under some willows near a bridge.

'Look at that temperature gauge! We'll have to let her cool down before I put some water in the radiator,' he said.

'Can we go down to the creek?' asked Boy.

'Shush!' said their mother. 'Don't wake Mamma.'

'It'll take a mag. nine quake to wake her up,' said the boys' dad.

As Boy and BB scrambled out of the back doors of the car, their grandmother, still sound asleep, sank down onto the back seat. I slid to the floor. The boys' mother reached over from the front seat and pulled the rug up to the old lady's chin. Only the top half of her head was sticking out.

Outside, I heard the boys' dad open the car boot. Luckily he found an empty tin can to collect some water in. 'You kids go ahead. We'll catch up,' he called.

With much shouting, the boys raced ahead of their mum and dad towards the bank that led down to the creek. But then I heard the two boys stop and run back towards their parents.

'Hey, look, those two men over there, on the other side of the bridge,' said Boy.

'Where did they come from?' asked the boys' dad.

'Maybe they're gypsies like in *Ruth Fielding*?' said Boy.

'Don't let your imagination run away with you,' said his mother.

I listened as the family slithered down the bank to the edge of the creek. The boys shrieked as they pulled off their shoes and socks and paddled into the cold water. The tin can gurgled when their dad plunged it into the creek and held it down to fill up. The boy's mum sat on a rock and slapped at a cloud of sandflies.

Above their heads, they would not have seen the two figures hurrying across the bridge to the car under the willows. But from where I was lying on the floor I could see between the front seats, and watched as two young men climbed in and quietly closed the car doors. The one in the driver's seat looked delighted to see the keys in the ignition. He yanked on the ignition button, and the old car burst into life. The planks on the bridge rattled as the car drove across it. And above the rattling of the planks the car's squeaky song sang out in the bright sunlit air.

I could imagine the fuss below.

'That sounds like our car!' shouted BB.

'It can't be,' said his father. 'I've got the keys in . . .' He plunged his hand into his empty pocket.

The boys, followed by their parents, scrambled up the bank and stood staring at the empty space beneath the willow trees.

'They've stolen our car!' said Boy.

'They've stolen your grandmother!' cried his mother.

'What about Teddy One-eye?' BB burst into tears.

The cloud of dust left by the stolen car blew back across

the bridge and drifted over the flummoxed family.

It was lucky they were on the main road to Invercargill, because I heard later it wasn't long before a freight truck turned up. Boy's father waved it down. The driver said he would telephone the police as soon as he got to the next petrol station.

In the stolen car, the driver had the accelerator pushed hard against the floor. He was crouching down, looking at the road through the steering wheel.

'Hey man, look at this! Stirling Moss!' he shouted. 'This little buzzer can really go!'

I hung on to the edge of the rug as the car swung around a corner on two wheels. A tall plume of dust billowed out from behind as the car swerved to miss a sheep that had strayed onto the road.

The boys' grandmother wasn't disturbed in the slightest by the car's antics, and I watched with my button eye as she slept on, snug as a bug under her rug.

With my other eye I saw that the temperature gauge was in the red again. If they didn't let the engine cool down soon, we would be in big trouble.

The Ford raced on. Its squeaky song became shrill and urgent.

Then, in the rear-vision mirror, the driver must have

noticed a dark shape forming on the road as the dust cleared near a corner. It was enough for him to see the outline of a police car. His mate opened his window and hung out to look behind them.

'Come on!' he shouted. 'Shake those snakes!'

The old car swung sideways and shot through an open gate into a newly ploughed field. It lurched and bumped across the furrows, and the two thieves were tossed around inside like rag dolls. Their heads hit the roof. I left the floor and jumped forward, lodging myself firmly between the two front seats. The driver glanced down. 'Goofy-looking bear,' he muttered, then took no further interest in me. But my glass eye with its excellent vision watched his every move. The car's song went from a shriek to a squeal.

This was exciting! There was far more excitement and fear in this adventure than any that Boy had taken me on.

The police car followed closely behind. At the far side of the field, the stolen car slid down the bank into a wide ditch full of water. Ducks scattered in a flurry of squawks and feathers. Now, much cooler, the old car churned up the bank on the opposite side as the two villains bounced off the side windows and hit the windscreen with their heads.

But, on the back seat, the old lady slept on.

The police car roared across the field like an angry bull.

It flew into the air and missed the ditch altogether, crash-landing, front wheels first on the opposite bank.

The Ford driver rammed his foot to the floor. The car catapulted towards a row of macrocarpa trees and squeezed through a narrow gap into a wheat field, then thrashed its way through the soft green of newly sprouted wheat.

'Ya-hoooooo!' shouted the young man in the passenger seat. 'The cops are still after us. Plant it, man!'

Ahead, a barn loomed up. The stolen car swerved to the left and went even faster — until it hit a haystack. A cloud of Rhode Island Reds exploded into the air.

The old car was buried in the middle of the stack, completely covered in hay. The driver couldn't see where he was going, but that didn't stop him. He drove even faster. The car feverishly screamed out its song.

On the back seat, the old lady slept on.

The driver of the stolen car turned on the windscreen wipers. Enough of the hay was swept away for him to get a glimpse of a farmer shouting and running out of his farmhouse, still clutching the cup of tea he had been drinking a few moments before. The driver yanked the wheel hard to the right and shot past the corner of the building, missing it by a whisker.

The police car, with its lights flashing and siren

screaming, followed in the tracks of the haystack.

The old lady slept on.

The speeding haystack drove across a flowerbed, swept aside a rose trellis, tore down a driveway and out onto the road.

'Plant ya boot, dude!' shouted the thief in the passenger seat.

'What'ya think I'm doing?' replied the driver.

The old Ford screamed in protest.

'Faster, go faster!'

And still the old lady slept on.

The car threw off the last of the hay and flew down the road like a bumblebee in a storm. But instead of continuing to gain speed, the Ford began to slow down. The squealing song became a squeaky one once more. Slower and slower went the car, until it stopped.

'Quick, get out! Cops'll be here in a minute!'

The two young men didn't get far. The police pulled alongside, scooped them up and threw them into the back seat of their car.

One of the policemen checked the dash of the stolen Ford. He then tied a towrope to its front bumper.

The old car was out of petrol.

'Thank you for returning our car,' said the boys' dad to the policeman. 'What do I owe you for the petrol?'

The boys' mother rushed to open the back door. Her mother woke, felt around for her handbag and threw back the rug.

'Are we in Lumsden already?' she asked.

'It's just down the road, Mum.'

The shadows were long and blue when they dropped the car off at the Kingston pub. The boy's dad and the old car had sung together all the way back home.

'Hope everyone had a good break,' said Vic Gherkin. As he slipped the car keys back into his pocket, he noticed his car was splattered with mud and several stalks of straw were caught under the windscreen wipers.

'We had a really exciting time,' said Boy.

His mother's eyebrows dropped just a little, but it was enough. Boy said no more. I kept quiet too. It was the best adventure I'd had for years.

'It was a corker outing,' added their grandmother. 'There's nothing like a Sunday drive to blow away the cobwebs.'

13
A GIRL'S BOOK

I HAD BEEN TO BOY'S SCHOOL many times. I had been to the school sports to watch Boy in a running race. I had watched as Boy and his friends ate sausages dripping with tomato sauce at a school break-up. And one year I even went to a school concert where Boy played a mouse in a play. This time it was Spring Festival Week and today was 'Favourite Toy Day'. Why Boy decided to take me, I don't know. It was probably to annoy BB. I certainly wasn't his favourite toy anymore, even though I wanted to be.

I was displayed with all the other toys at the front of the room. Each child gave a morning talk about their toy and why they chose to bring it along. No sooner had Boy started to speak about me than he was drowned out by laughter. The other children thought he had brought me along as a joke. He probably had. I had seen him grinning as he was getting ready to take me to school that morning. My tattered fur and patched body looked shabby beside the other toys. And when Boy said my name was Teddy One-eye, the room exploded.

After the toy talks, I spent the rest of the day sitting on top of the book cupboard, waiting to go home.

At three o'clock, Boy put his chair up on his desk and hurriedly said, 'Good afternoon Mr McLeod.' He stuffed me into his bag. As he jumped from the school porch onto the path, we heard, 'I know something that you don't.'

'I haven't got time for that, Frankie,' said Boy. 'I've got to get home.'

'But I know something real good,' said Frankie Gibbs.

'Well, it won't be as good as what I'm going to hear. My grandma is reading me a book. And it's really exciting!'

'What's so good about a book?' asked Frankie.

'Come and find out.'

The two boys raced down the hill and across the stretch of rough ground to the railway line. Boy was ahead. Frankie stumbled along behind. With one hand he tried to stop his school bag from banging against his back, while with the other he managed to poke a sandwich left over from his lunch into his mouth. At the railway line they turned towards Boy's house. The afternoon train from Invercargill was due any minute. But if the boys were quick, they would be home before it came down the tracks behind them.

Boy's grandmother had been waiting. But now she was asleep. Her chin on her chest. Her hands in a basin of gooseberries that she had been topping and tailing. The book lay next to her. Boy's mother was in the garden. The kettle was softly singing on the coal range. Everything was perfect for a story.

'I brought Frankie with me.'

The old lady woke up. 'That's fine,' she said. 'Do you boys want a piece?'

'No thanks,' said Frankie, wiping his mouth with the sleeve of his jersey. 'Just had a sandwich.'

'I'll get something later, thanks,' said Boy.

The 3.20 from Invercargill rattled past the gate.

'That won't do the washing any good,' said the old lady

as she looked up to see a cloud of black smoke drift past the kitchen window.

'Mamma . . . story please,' said Boy.

'How did your morning talk go?' asked his grandmother. She put the basin of gooseberries on the floor to finish later.

'Okay, I s'pose,' said Boy. 'But everyone laughed at Teddy One-eye—'

His grandmother frowned. 'Where is Teddy?'

Boy pulled me from his bag and sat me beside his grandmother. She pulled me close to her. Then Boy sat down next to me. Frankie found a seat by the window. I suspected he was hedging his bets. If the story turned out to be a fizzer, he could watch what was happening down by the engine shed. I put Frankie out of my mind and focused my best eye on the book so I could follow the words.

Boy's grandmother smiled. She opened the book and carefully put the three pieces of red wool on the arm of the sofa. She adjusted her glasses. She cleared her throat.

'Now,' she said, '*Chapter Seven: Fellow Travellers . . .*'

Tom stayed outside to do some repairs on the car while Ruth and Helen went into the old abandoned house to shelter from the oncoming storm and to make a cup of tea on their portable stove.

'"What a lonesome, eerie sort of place," shivered Helen.'

They heard a noise and thought it was Tom coming inside, but it was two gypsy men. Helen and Ruth quickly hid in another room and listened as the gypsies plotted to rob the Gypsy Queen Zelaya of her treasure. The girls managed to frighten the men away by disturbing some bats that flew out of the chimney and into the room.

Tom finished fixing the car and the three friends left the old house to continue their journey. But . . .

'Right at the foot of a hill, and by the shore of a dark lake, the engine died.'

There was nothing else for it: Tom would have to walk to Severn Corners to get help.

The two girls stayed in the car out of the rain. It began to get dark. Through the gloom the girls watched 'a string of odd-looking wagons moving along the narrow trail down by the lake's edge.'

The two girls in the car were soon spotted, and several 'strange-looking people — all swarthy, dark-haired and red-lipped' — came up the hill to see them.

A pleasant young woman with a baby on her hip offered to take Helen and Ruth to Severn Corners in her caravan.

'Ruth felt some doubt about going with the woman. She was so dark and foreign looking.'

The girls finally decided to take up the offer of a lift. They followed the woman down to the lakeside where '*a green van, horses and a handsome driver*' were waiting.

Helen and Ruth climbed aboard. To their horror they saw '*an old, old crone, sitting on a stool, bent forward with her sharp chin resting on her clenched fists, while her iron-grey elf-locks hung about her wrinkled, nut-brown face.*'

The old woman was Queen Zelaya and she was interested to hear that the girls had their own car. She said, '"*Then your parents are wealthy,*" *and the fangs in her mouth displayed themselves in a dreadful smile. "It is fine to be rich. The poor gypsy scarcely knows where to lay her head, but you little ladies have great houses and much money — eh?*"'

Queen Zelaya made Helen and Ruth her prisoners. Instead of going to Severn Corners, they arrived in a gypsy camp. The girls were forced to sleep in the same caravan as the queen. They pretended to go to sleep but secretly watched while the old crone rummaged through her boxes of money and jewels. She spent a great deal of time admiring a beautiful pearl necklace.

I read along with Boy's grandmother. Boy sat beside me, as still as a stone. But Frankie, on his chair, was stretching and yawning. He was finding it difficult to sit still.

The story continued. It became even more exciting.

Next morning, the two girls were allowed to go down to the river to wash. This was their chance to escape. They found a fishing punt, and Helen managed to get away. But Ruth was caught and taken back to the queen's caravan. The old crone was very angry.

'*The queen took some walnut stain and sponged Ruth's face and neck, her arms, hands and legs. She threw some earth on Ruth's feet. She gave her a torn and dirty frock to put on. "Now," hissed the old woman, "if they come to search for you we will say you are ours — an orphan gypsy, wicked through and through."*'

'Seven chapters!' said Boy's grandmother. 'I'm exhausted!'

So was I. My glass eye had been working overtime to keep up with the words as they danced all over the page.

'Did you enjoy that, Frankie?' asked the old lady.

'Not much,' replied Frankie.

'Why not?' asked Boy.

'It's a girl's book,' he said.

'It was my mum's,' said Boy.

'Yeah,' said Frankie. 'Your mum's a girl — or was.'

Boy became quiet.

'Better go. Mum O'Donnell will be wondering where I am.' Frankie jumped up, glad to be able to escape at long last. 'See ya!'

Boy said nothing.

The next day, the 3.20 from Invercargill roared past the house before he got home from school. When Boy came into the kitchen, his grandmother and I were waiting.

'Would you like a bit more *Ruth Fielding*?' asked his grandmother.

'Nah. Thanks. I think I'll go over and play with the Kariannis kids.'

14
LISLE STOCKINGS

THIS YEAR, IT WAS DECIDED, there had been enough going on in Kingston. There had been parties for the coronation, do's at the pub to celebrate Everest, and Archie McCain had a big three-course dinner for his fiftieth. Every man and his dog had been invited. To have a big bonfire with a guy as well as all the fireworks would be too much.

'Guy Fawkes night,' said the boys' dad, 'would be just as good with a few crackers down at the railway station.'

Mrs Hume was having afternoon tea with the boys' mother. I was on the floor behind the couch where BB had left me.

'I think it is a good idea to forget about a bonfire this year,' said Mrs Hume. 'I've asked the Four Square in Lumsden to send up a few fireworks on the freight truck. That'll be enough.'

'I've done the same,' said the boys' mum. 'The kids get too excited. It won't hurt to have a quiet Guy Fawkes this year.'

But the Kingston kids were just as excited as every other year. In a scary sort of way, they liked being dwarfed by the mountain of fire down on the beach. And they liked the cheeky guy when he tried to escape. But most of all they liked the fireworks. The Catherine Wheels, the Tom Thumbs, and the colourful ones, Mt Vesuvius, the Flower Pots and Golden Rain. A Guy Fawkes night without a bonfire and a guy just this once would be okay, they supposed.

Bangers and mash with cabbage from the garden, followed by junket and bottled plums, was gobbled up by the two boys so quickly it almost made my glass eye water to watch them.

'We're ready!' shouted the little boy as he dropped his

spoon into his empty plate.

Their grandmother said nothing, but she looked at him in a way that said, 'You'll be ready when I say so.'

The little boy saw the look. He slid off his chair and joined his big brother in clearing the table.

'Can we go now?' asked the older boy when they'd finished the dishes.

His mother looked at the clock above the range. 'It won't be dark for ages yet,' she said. 'Besides, have you done your homework?'

'Mr McLeod didn't give us any because of Guy Fawkes.'

'Well, all right. We won't be able to stay late anyway, because your little brother will need to go to bed. Put your coat on. There'll be a cold wind.'

'Can I take Teddy One-eye?' asked BB.

At the mention of that name, his grandmother looked up. 'He'd be better at home,' she said.

BB bawled. 'But he likes fireworks!'

His mother let out a long sigh. 'You've already lost him once. And I'm not looking after him.'

The little boy put his coat on and tucked me under his arm.

'Just a minute,' said the boys' grandmother. 'I can't be seen out wearing these old stockings.'

The old lady went into her room. She came back wearing her new lisle stockings, the ones she kept for best.

The grandmother, the mother, the two boys and I set off along the gravel at the side of the railway line towards the station. The boys' dad was already there. He had collected their bag of fireworks off the freight truck that afternoon. When he saw us coming, he lit a Tom Thumb on his roll-your-own and threw it across the tracks. The boys shrieked with delight. But their grandmother stopped. She stood, swaying slightly, holding her walking stick in front of her with both hands.

'I think I might go back home,' she said.

'You'll be okay. Come and sit in here out of the wind,' said the boys' mother. She helped the old lady into the open-fronted railway-station waiting room. 'You'll see everything from here.'

The boys were jumping up and down with excitement.

'Can I light something, can I?' asked the little boy, swinging me backwards and forwards between his legs.

'Have you got some matches?' said his father.

'No.'

'I think that's your answer then,' said his dad.

The Humes arrived, walking down the road in a line like cows off to the milking shed. Then the Bells scrambled across the tracks from the house by the lake. Other families trickled along. Everyone had bags of fireworks. They put them into a heap inside the stationmaster's office.

'Grab some of these crackers, kids,' said Mr Bell. 'We'll keep the coloured ones till it gets dark.' He handed out strings of Tom Thumbs and Double Happies. Walter Hume, who was almost twelve, was put in charge of the matches.

Single explosions followed by a series of bangs like a machine-gun echoed around the railway station as the kids threw crackers at one another. The boys' grandmother peered through a pall of smoke as it drifted past the waiting room. Her eyes were wide, her mouth pursed to a slit.

Even though the sun had almost set behind the Hector mountains, the southern evening sky was still bright. The tops of the poplars at the edge of the lake, clipped by the last rays, were gleaming gold. Further down, in the shadows, the spring-green leaves fluttered like tiny flags in the cold breeze.

Some of the smallest children were yawning.

'Someone here is asleep on his feet,' said the boys' mother. She picked up her littlest boy and sat him on her hip. I hung from his hand, my feet almost touching the platform.

BB's mum carried him into the waiting room and sat

next to the grandmother. As the little boy fell asleep on her knee, his grip relaxed and I fell to the floor. I landed so that my glass eye looked out across the platform and my button eye peered up into the sky. Erratic explosions kept coming from behind us as the kids chased each other down the road towards the pub.

In the meantime, the boys' father had sorted through the bags of fireworks and found three Catherine Wheels. With a hammer and nails from the toolbox in the stationmaster's office, he nailed them to the wall near the waiting room.

'Hey kids! Catherine Wheel time!'

The kids came panting back along the road. Some of them took off their coats and threw them into the waiting room.

Boy's father took the cigarette from his lips and held it to the twist of paper under the first of the three Catherine Wheels on the wall.

It fizzed and sparked, and then the fire took hold. A torrent of stars shot out and forced the wheel to start spinning. Even in the dusky light it was spectacular. The Catherine Wheel whizzed round and round, faster and faster. Billions of tiny sparks flew into the air and onto the platform. The firework lit the young and old watching faces with equal intensity. Frown lines, weary eyes, weathered cheeks were wiped away. Parents looked as young as their children. And then the spinning wheel of sparks slowed, the light faded and the little whizzer dribbled to a stop. Parents looked like parents again.

There was a burst of applause and cries of 'Wow!' and 'Gee whizz!'

It was getting darker. It would soon be dark enough to light the Skyrockets, the Flower Pots and the Roman Candles. But — there were two more Catherine Wheels. The first one had been a big hit. Parents pushed their kids in front of them to get a better look.

Boy's father reached forward once more with his cigarette. If one Catherine Wheel caused that much excitement, imagine what two would do. He poked his cigarette under the next wheel and waited a few seconds before moving to the one beside it. The first one spluttered and spat, then burst into life — a blur of blinding light. Then it flew off the nail and spun up into the air. It rivalled the sun with its brilliance. But it was in the air for only a moment before it fell onto the platform. On the ground, it took off like a comet, spinning among the feet of the onlookers and into the waiting room. Instantly, the room was as bright as midday. The wheel raced across the floor and hit the far wall. On impact, it changed direction and made its way towards where I was lying on the floor. Still spinning madly and shooting millions of sparks, it hit my back, leapt into the air, jumped over my head and fell down in front of my face.

But it didn't stop there. It sped towards the legs of the boys' grandmother. She struggled to her feet. But she was not quick enough. The Catherine Wheel began to circle her legs as she tried to get out of its way. She lashed at it with her walking stick. But still it followed her. She hobbled out onto the platform while the fiery little wheel nipped at her legs like a yappy fox terrier. Then, quite quickly, the wheel spent itself, and collapsed in a tiny, exhausted heap at her feet. She looked down at her best pair of lisle stockings. They were full of holes.

The third wheel was now spinning wildly on the wall. Faces turned from the old lady and once more were washed by the fountain of youth. While they watched, this wheel, too, fell from the wall. It rolled, still spitting sparks, across the platform, through the door of the stationmaster's office, towards the bags of fireworks that had been stored in there for safe-keeping.

The Catherine Wheel quickly burnt its way into the first bag. Mr Bell rushed into his office. He stamped on the bag, but he was too late. The burning firework was igniting all the other fireworks. He picked the bags up and threw them outside, over the heads of the families gathered on the platform. In mid-air, the bags exploded. Skyrockets zoomed above the little crowd. Some flew up and out over the lake; others went straight up into the air above the railway station. Roman Candles, Screaming Banshees, Flower Pots, Golden Showers and a super-sized Mt Vesuvius sprayed the crowd with a torrent of sparks and tiny lumps of fire. Boom Boxes, Power Bombs and Mighty Thunders added bass notes to the mighty performance.

People were quick to get out of the way of the golden, red and green rain. Some dived off the platform onto the railway tracks with their hands over their heads. Mrs Hume grabbed two of her kids and ran across the road and hid in some willows. Mrs Bell opened her coat and engulfed a small child standing next to her. Others ran towards the pub where the lights had been switched on early. Mr Bell, welded to the spot, watched the display through his office door. And Boy's dad stood scratching his head, wondering why the nails hadn't held the Catherine Wheels more securely. His face was covered with black smoke smuts. The crown of his hat was on fire.

Then it was all over. Some Tom Thumbs exploded, adding a string of full-stops. The boys' mother came out of the waiting room, carrying her sleeping child. Boy ran to join her.

'Wow! Wasn't that great!' he said. 'That was much better than a bonfire.'

I was on the floor. My back was smouldering where the Catherine Wheel had hit me, but I didn't care. I hadn't had such an exciting adventure since I was kidnapped in the stolen car.

Boy picked me up, and then his dad, who had managed to put his hat out by dipping it in the fire bucket, picked us both up and hugged us.

'That was certainly one out of the box,' said Mr Bell. 'There's a hell of a mess, but I'll come over in the morning and clean it up.'

The parents gathered their kids and slowly made their way across the carpet of coloured paper and dead fireworks. The clatter of spent skyrockets landing on the station roof was replaced by the sound of soft rain.

'Where's Mamma?' asked the boys' mother.

Boy pointed up the railway line towards their house. The old lady was feeling her way with her walking stick along the tracks. There was just enough light to see her legs. From where we were standing, it looked as if she was wearing brown stockings with white polka dots.

Next day, the boy burst through the back door as the 3.20 raced passed the house. His grandmother was sitting on a chair by the window in the kitchen.

'What are you doing, Mamma?' asked the boy.

'I'm mending my stockings. The ones the Catherine Wheels burnt holes in last night,' she said. 'I won't be able to wear them on the bus to go home. They'll have to be my second-best ones now.'

'Third-best,' said the boy.

'That's right, I've already got a pair for second-best.' She laughed. 'I'll send to Lumsden for a new pair before I go back to Invercargill.'

15
GOOD TIMING

IT HAD BEEN A LONG YEAR, but at last it was Christmas Eve. You could taste the excitement in the air as if it were candy floss.

The two brothers hung pillowcases on each side of the coal range. On the hearth they placed one of their mother's good plates with a slice of Christmas cake on it. Nearby were a glass, a bottle of beer and an opener. Two weeks ago the family had decorated the kitchen with crêpe-paper streamers and home-made paper lanterns. Christmas cards covered the mantelpiece. The ones that couldn't fit there were pinned to the curtains.

'How will Santa get down the chimney if the coal range is in the way?' asked BB. It was the first year that this had concerned him.

'Don't worry,' said his big brother. 'Santa has keys to all the houses in the world. He'll just come through the back door.'

The boys' mother had filled the tins with slices and biscuits and cupcakes. The fruit for the Christmas cake had soaked in ginger ale for days before being baked into a rich, dark slab that was so heavy it could barely be lifted out of the baking tin. The boys' grandmother made jam from the strawberries in the garden. On Christmas Eve she podded peas and beans, and did what she always did if she was around — plucked the chook for Christmas dinner. She would have chopped its head off too if her arthritic fingers had been able to grip the axe.

Christmas Day started early. The summer sun filled the house with light at such an early hour that even if the boys had wanted to sleep in, they couldn't. Of course they wouldn't. They were far too excited to stay in bed until the adults woke. BB scooped me up from the floor, then he and Boy charged into the kitchen.

Their grandmother was already up, stoking the fire to make an early morning cuppa.

'Mamma, did you eat the cake?' asked Boy.

'And Merry Christmas to you too,' was her reply. She added, 'No, I certainly did not.'

'It was Santa Claus, stupid!' said BB. 'And he drank the beer too.'

The older boy looked at the plate covered in crumbs and noticed the empty beer bottle. He wasn't convinced. He had been having doubts about Christmas things lately. But he decided not to say anything that might stop the flow of presents he expected and enjoyed every year.

The baby brother tossed me onto the couch, then lifted his bulging pillowcase down onto the floor. He tipped it upside down. A tall tin crane called Reacher, with a handle to wind up the bucket, landed on the mat. It was followed by a book about wild animals in Africa, a pair of navy-blue bathing togs with an anchor stitched onto the front, a peppermint-candy walking stick, and a pack of Happy Families cards. An orange rolled off under the couch, and a small bag of nuts in the shell fell neatly into the bucket of the crane. The little boy quickly picked up the candy stick, tore off the cellophane and poked the stick into his mouth.

The older boy carefully reached into his bag and drew out a big box. He placed it on the table. He undid two little clips and lifted the lid. Three rows of coloured pencils were lined up in sequence: Prussian blue, ultramarine, cobalt, turquoise, cerulean. And then came the greens — viridian, olive, forest green, emerald, chartreuse and mint — followed by the yellows, the browns, oranges, reds and violets. The boy smiled to himself, closed the lid of the pencil box and snibbed it shut. He climbed onto a chair by the range and moved two Christmas cards on the mantelpiece. I watched as Boy reached up and placed the box behind the black stone clock.

'He won't be able to get them there,' I heard him say to himself.

He climbed back down and spread the rest of his Christmas presents over the table — *Cole's Funny Picture Book No.2*, a *Chatterbox* annual, some black bathing togs with a white belt, a sunhat, a game of Donkey, a candy walking stick, an orange and some nuts. He broke a piece off the candy stick. He peeled the orange and shoved it into his mouth while he sucked the candy. He looked slowly over his gifts before making them into a neat stack and carrying them into his bedroom.

'Come on, kids, get dressed,' shouted their father as he

came into the room, yawning and scratching his mop of unruly hair. 'How about some breakfast, Mum?' he asked the boys' grandmother. 'What do you fancy?'

'Anything, as long as it's not too fatty,' she replied.

I had seen his breakfasts many times before. This morning it was to be one of his favourites — lamb's fry and bacon. And eggs, of course, and fried bread and home-made tomato sauce. It was good for you, he claimed, when anyone suggested otherwise. 'Well, the sauce is made from our own tomatoes.'

By mid-morning, every corner of the house was filled with the smells of food. Memories of the fried liver and bacon dallied in the pantry. In the kitchen, they had been ousted by the heady aroma of roasted chicken and lamb — a delicious scent that made your mouth fill with saliva in anticipation. In the coolest part of the house, the bathroom, fruit salads, trifle and jelly were giving off their own delicate veils of smell. And, even though all the windows and the front and back doors had been thrown open to invite the sunny summer's day inside, other more remote parts of the house had their own smells too. The boys' bedroom recalled the oranges and peppermint candy that had been devoured at daybreak. In the parents' bedroom, the air had a tinge of perfume from the bottle that was opened only for something special. And last of all, the grandmother's bedroom, just off the kitchen. It collected all of the smells in a confusing concoction. If the old lady hadn't lost her sense of smell, it would have given her a headache. And in that bedroom, lurking beneath the smells of the roast meat, the trifles, fruit salads and the morning's breakfast, was the illicit smell of sherry. The boys' father had bought a bottle of Penfold's Sweet Sherry in Garston. Christmas was the only time of the year the old lady had 'something to drink'. She had quietly sipped the sweet wine as she sat on her bed with the door closed. She didn't want the boys to see her drinking. It would be a bad influence.

After dinner at midday, the afternoon grew lazy and fat. A mellow breeze floated across the tops of the willows by the creek and through the back door. The parents sat slumped, unable to move. They had eaten too much. They did it every Christmas and swore they wouldn't do it again. The boys' grandmother had gone for a walk down to the gate. BB was in the back yard, playing with his new crane, and Boy lay on his bed reading his new *Cole's Funny Picture Book*.

The boys' father stretched an arm across his full stomach and turned on the radio to get the news. A few moments of static cleared to reveal the final bars of 'God Rest Ye Merry Gentlemen' sung by the choir of the Wellington Cathedral. Now there was to be a special broadcast from Waiouru by the Prime Minister.

'Thank goodness Mum's not here,' said the boys' mother. 'She would hit the radio with her walking stick. She can't stand Sid Holland.'

'Ssshhhh!' said the boys' father. 'He's talking about something that's happened.'

'*It is with profound regret that I have to announce that a most serious railway accident has occurred to the 3 p.m. express travelling from Wellington to Auckland . . .*' The broadcast was suddenly swamped by static.

The Prime Minister's voice came back. '*The disaster occurred at 10.21 p.m. last night, three-quarters of a mile north of Tangiwai . . .*' Again static cut in.

'Barbara! She was on the train to Auckland last night!'

The boys' mother jumped up and thumped the top of the radio.

The PM came back. '*As far as can be ascertained, an enormous volume of water swept down the river . . .*'

The PM was gone again.

The boys' grandmother came through the front door and down the hall.

'Come and listen to the Prime Minister, Mum,' called their mother.

'Over my dead body,' replied the old lady. 'I hate his guts!'

'But Barbara could have been on that train!'

The old woman paused. There was something in her daughter's voice that said this was serious. Without saying another word, she made her way across the room and lowered herself into a chair near the radio.

As if the radio had cleared its throat, the Prime Minister's voice came back.

'*This is the most disastrous railway accident in New Zealand's history . . . it has been attended by an appalling loss of life.*'

The boys' grandmother drew in a deep breath, half-gulp, half-sob.

'*Some bodies have been recovered fifteen miles from the scene of the disaster. I gravely fear that there is little hope of further persons being rescued alive.*'

That was all they heard. The radio delivered a continuous stream of static.

The boys' father slowly stood up and turned the radio off.

A cool draught from the lake flowed through the front door. The paper lanterns lifted and fell. A rustling ran through the crêpe-paper streamers, and three Christmas cards toppled off the mantelpiece onto the hearth. The warmth of the family's Christmas was carried out the back door by the cool air, over the paddocks behind the house, to join the memories of Christmases past.

'I must find out if my sister is all right,' cried the boys' mother. 'I'm going down to the Bells to use their phone.'

'What good's that?' asked the boys' father. 'You can't ring Barbara. They don't have a phone.'

'No, but I can send a telegram.' She took off her apron and headed to the back door.

'No one will be working today. It's Christmas Day!'

But she didn't hear him. She was already hurrying down the gravel path at the side of the house.

The house cooled quickly. The old lady moved from room to room, closing windows and shutting doors. The sky turned grey. It cast a gloomy light, a light that seemed to shrivel the Christmas decorations and leach them of colour. The boys' father shovelled some coal into the range and pushed the kettle into the centre to boil. When the boys' mother returned, she came in and sat down without saying a word.

The afternoon dragged on. The three adults drank cup after cup of tea. BB brought his crane inside and played with it on the floor in the hall. A plate of Christmas cake sat untouched on the table beside Boy as he made a drawing with his new coloured pencils of a windmill with outstretched arms.

'I sent the telegram to the Clarksons next door to where Barbara's staying.' The boys' mother looked at her mother. 'Just in case Barbara was on that—' She burst into tears.

BB ran to his mother and buried his head in her lap. His big brother didn't look up. He was too busy colouring a tiny detail on one of the sails of his windmill. Their mother found a handkerchief up the sleeve of her blouse and blew her nose. Then she took a loud slurp of tea.

'We've done all we can do. We'll just have to wait,' said the boys' father. 'The Queen's Christmas Message is on soon.'

'I don't want to hear it.'

'It's the first time one has been delivered from New Zealand.'

'I don't care. I just want to hear my sister's safe.'

Yet another pot of tea was brewed. The boys put on jerseys and went outside to make a hut. The old lady went to her bedroom and closed the door. The boys' father took a thriller by Carter Brown off a high shelf. Usually the boys' mother objected to these books, but today she took no notice. She was trying to convince everyone that she was absorbed in an article in the *Woman's Weekly*. But her mind was racing, overflowing with 'what-ifs'. A large blowfly was eyeing the slices of Christmas cake that remained untouched on the table.

At 5.30 the boys' mother stood up. 'I'd better get something for the boys' tea.' She went to the pantry and took an old carving knife from a drawer. She opened the back door and walked across the yard to the vegetable garden to cut a lettuce to make a salad.

The boys' father looked up from his book when something caught his eye through the window. He stood up and looked out to see what it was. John Bell was standing talking to his wife. He could see by the way her beaming face lit up the grey afternoon that she was listening to good news. John Bell turned and ran back down the path. The boys' mother came hurrying inside.

'She was on the train the night before! She's sitting in Auckland, safe and sound.'

The old lady came out of her room, a handkerchief screwed into the palm of her hand. BB came running into the kitchen.

'Hey Mum, you dropped your lettuce.'

She turned, grabbed both her sons and hugged them to her. She cried until the tears began to wet their hair.

16
THE READER
1954

I GOT BETTER AND BETTER at reading. I read everything and read everywhere. I read over shoulders. I read
under arms, on people's laps and while I was lying on the
floor. I read by daylight, by moonlight or by the light of a
candle. I read inside, outside, on the train and on the bus.

Sometimes it was hard to read upside down —

THE ROYAL TOUR OF NZ

DUKE QUEEN'S CHAUFFEUR FOR 28 MILES OF DRIVE

(P.A.)   TE KAUWHATA, December 30.

For 28 miles today, the Duke of Edinburgh was the Queen's chauffeur from Pukekohe to Te Kauwhata. The Duke, who has earned the reputation of an accomplished driver, set a spanking pace for the royal entourage.

Two miles beyond Pukekohe the royal procession unexpectedly halted. The Queen and the Duke transferred from their landaulette to an open tourer-type Daimler. The Duke sat at the wheel and the Queen occupied the front seat beside him.

In Britain, The Duke often drives the Queen when they are out on private runs but until today he has not taken the wheel in a Royal procession.

Whenever a group of people had gathered at a roadside, the Duke slowed the pace of the car so that they should all get a glimpse of the Queen.

Six miles from Alton Lodge, the procession slowed and came almost to a halt as if the Queen and Duke were to return to their original car. However, after no more than a momentary pause the cars drove on with the duke still at the wheel.

Or sideways —

New Version Of Walter Raleigh Act

(P.A.) PUKEKOHE, Dec. 30

This Raleigh tradition dies hard.

Today, near Paerata the royal car approached a group of about 30 people. Among them were two men who laid their jackets on the road. The Royal car duly passed over them - so did the other dozen cars of the Royal entourage.

Often, while sprawled on the floor or propped up on the sofa, I read snippets of news in the *Southland Times* before being whisked away for a ride in BB's truck or taken to bed for a nap. If I managed to end up back in the same place, hoping to read more of a particular newspaper article, I might find that the paper had already been used to wrap up potato peelings or to light the fire. My head was filled with unfinished stories.

And on top of the pile of stories to be finished was the adventure that poor Ruth Fielding was having. She was still in the clutches of the Gypsy Queen. I *had* to find out what happened next.

Boy had lost interest. He didn't want to be seen, especially by his best friend, to be enjoying a book written for girls.

His grandmother had left the book in his bedroom and it remained unopened on the chest of drawers under the window. I was often dumped next to it. How I ached to be able to pull the red wool hard enough to open those big soft pages and continue reading. Ruth and her friends and all those gypsies were alive in there. But they were frozen to the spot, waiting to be given the order to continue their adventure. If only I could start reading the words that would bring them back to life!

Then, one very warm day, everything fell into place. My wish came true.

BB was playing with me in the bedroom when his aunt and uncle from Alexandra arrived for a surprise visit. He jumped up when he heard them talking in the kitchen. He pushed me roughly onto the chest of drawers where the book lay and ran from the room.

One of my feet pressed hard against the pages. The force was enough to push the book open. I could see the words on the broad, creamy pages clearly with my glass eye. But it was the wrong page. The strands of red wool, where the adventure was poised to start, were buried several pages down.

Just as I was beginning to feel sorry for myself, a stiff breeze hurried through the open window and turned a page.

The breeze continued to blow. Another page turned. And another. Until the page opened where the red wool lay.

Chapter Fourteen: Roberto Again.

I started to read. Ruth and the gypsies sprang to life. My foot held the page until I was ready to read the next one. All afternoon the breeze rustled through the book, and I gobbled up the story like a hungry bear coming out of hibernation.

Ruth was taken to a secret gypsy camp on an island in the middle of the lake. And, luckily, Helen was saved by Tom from the rapids. The following night Roberto drugged his grandmother, Queen Zelaya, and helped Ruth escape and return to the Red Mill. The next day, the gypsies left the island hideout and fled to another hiding place.

A week later, Ruth and Helen left for the new term at Briarwood Hall. On the train they heard of a new girl whose wealthy aunt had a fine pearl necklace, worth at least $50,000, stolen by some gypsies. It sounded like the one Ruth had seen in the hands of Queen Zelaya. There was a reward of $5,000 for its return.

Helen's father visited the girls at Briarwood. He took them out in his car for a drive and happened to pass Roberto the gypsy boy, who was up a tree, knocking down chestnuts. As they watched, he fell and was badly hurt. They took him to a hospital, hoping he would tell them where the gypsies were hiding. But when he gained consciousness, he couldn't speak.

Roberto's broken bones gradually mended, and Ruth got him a job as an assistant gardener at Briarwood. She hoped to find where the gypsies had gone and claim the reward for the pearl necklace so she could return the $50 that Uncle Jabez had given her.

One night a candle set light to a curtain. Roberto climbed the fire escape and put the fire out. When Ruth told him she was worried about his burnt hands, Roberto spoke. It was clear he had been fooling everyone.

The girls sent a telegram to Mr Cameron, Helen's father. He came the next day and took Roberto to New York where he helped the police track down the band of gypsies. The old Gypsy Queen was deported to Bohemia, the pearl necklace was recovered and the $5,000 reward was put into Ruth's bank account. Roberto gave up his gypsy ways. He cut his hair, removed his earrings, put on a smart grey suit and became an American.

Ruth returned to school just in time for her next adventure.

I lay soaking in the afternoon sun as it streamed through the window. I could hear the excited chattering out in the kitchen. The boys were telling their aunt and uncle about their trip to Queenstown on the *Earnslaw*. They talked about the bakery where they ate mutton pies and Boston buns. I was not envious of their feast. Teddy bears can't eat, but I felt as if I had just finished a plate of steak and kidney stew with dumplings, followed by a bowl of steamed pudding and ice cream. Reading a good story filled me up just like a big dinner.

17
OUT IN THE COLD

TWO YEARS ROLLED BY. I noticed BB was also losing interest in me. I was becoming invisible. Each day I vanished a little more from his world. I was left on the end of his bed and did not move from there except for when I was shifted to the chest of drawers or onto the floor each morning when his bed was made.

Then one day I made the move I was not ready for. I was taken to The Trunk, the place I had heard mentioned with dread by some of the other toys. I had seen The Trunk as I passed by with one of the boys, but I had never thought I would ever end up there. The Trunk was the home of unwanted toys. Toys no longer loved, no longer of interest to anyone in the family. As a gesture to the adoration I'd once enjoyed, the boy's mother wrapped me in an old cot blanket before placing (throwing) me inside.

The family told themselves that The Trunk was a wonderful place, full of wonderful things for little children to play with when they came to visit. Actually, it was a graveyard, a bone house, a dumping ground. If a child ever wondered where old toys went when they were no longer loved, it was here, in the old tin trunk smelling of damp and rust that sat on the front veranda looking over the railway line to the glittering lake surrounded by majestic poplars that turned to gold in the autumn. It sounded idyllic, but it wasn't. The toys could not see the view. The lid of the trunk was always closed and the interior was dark except for a few rays of light that squeezed through the rust holes. When these faded and disappeared, you knew it was night time.

My position in the trunk was uncomfortable. I was rammed head-first beside Mr Gee, a wind-up doll from the Caribbean whose legs still danced to an old carnival tune that played endlessly in his head. My glorious glass eye stared into Mr Gee's black face. My button eye was caught in the rigging of Reacher, the battered tin crane BB had got for Christmas some years earlier. On my back sat a box of wooden blocks with the colour chewed off.

Days and nights melted until I could no longer tell how long I had been there. There were times when the rain, beating on the battered lid of the trunk, deafened us with its roar. Or the sun would heat the tin walls until the trunk became an oven. Seasons slipped by without anyone opening the trunk until one day I realised it must be spring. I could smell the lilac blooming by the back gate. That meant the front and back doors of the house were open. And when I heard a voice saying, 'I had a lovely ride up on the bus, thank you. The driver was very nice,' I knew it was definitely springtime. The boys' grand-mother had come for a visit.

18
THE NIGHT VISITOR

THAT NIGHT, WELL AFTER the last trickle of light had faded from the rust holes, I heard a snuffling noise and a scrape of claws on the wooden floor of the veranda. The latch on the trunk squeaked. Someone or something was trying to lift it. It squeaked again, and then made a clunk as it fell back against the lid. I was aware of the trunk being opened but, lying on my face, I couldn't see who was doing it. Perhaps one of the boys had decided I should be his friend again and my rightful place was in his bed? My heart started beating with excitement.

The box of blocks was pushed off my back and a tiny hand grabbed my blanket. I was tossed into the air. When I landed, I hit the veranda floor and rolled down the steps to the gravel path. I landed on my back and watched with both eyes, glass and button, as a small furry shape reached into the trunk and pulled out Mr Gee. With his feet still sambaing to the salsa beat, he was thrown onto the path as well. Reacher the crane followed, and just missed my head. It collapsed in a jumbled heap.

Board books, a blue flannel dog and one wooden block at a time came next. The din echoed around the garden and through the house. The front door opened and the boys' father in his pyjamas shone a torch into the trunk.

Sitting in the middle of the remaining toys was a possum. For a moment it was frozen in the light, then it jumped and sprang over the veranda railing, scampered across the lawn and up into the willow trees at the side of the house.

'What on earth is going on?' The boys' grandmother, wrapped in her pink candlewick dressing gown, appeared in the doorway.

'A beast got into the toy trunk,' said the boys' father.

'I thought you lot didn't believe in beasts anymore,' said the old lady. A tiny smile trembled at the corner of her mouth.

'Well, this one was real all right.'

The old lady looked at the heap of toys. 'Is that Teddy down there on the gravel?' She grabbed hold of the torch and pointed it down the steps. 'What's he doing out here?'

The boys' father did not answer for a moment and then said, 'Old Teddy One-eye? The kids have finished with him.'

'He's been in The Trunk?' she asked. 'He deserves to be looked after! And don't call him that awful name!'

The old lady carefully descended the steps and picked me up. She tucked me under one arm and, with her stick in her other hand, climbed back onto the veranda. Walking slowly, almost as if I was asleep and should not be woken, she took me to her bedroom and placed me on top of the sewing machine in front of the window by her bed.

And there I stayed, on my own, in grand isolation. No one dared move me. No one dared touch me. Even after the boys' grandmother went back to Invercargill, no one came into that room. She had made it quite clear I was special and should be taken care of. She said no more than that.

At the window, propped up, body forward, with my forehead against the glass, I watched with my mismatched eyes as hawks and leaves of yellow chased clouds across the sky. At night, after the wind had swept the sky clear, the Southern Cross once more hung like a crown high above my head. It shone brighter than all the other stars and seemed to promise better things to come. How long that would take, it did not say.

As I wondered about this, a large grey moth struck the window. It fluttered madly against my head, with only the windowpane separating us. Again and again it struck the glass with the force of a powder puff. Was it trying to tell me something? Or trying to remind me of something I should remember? Something from long ago?

I sat undisturbed for many months until one morning the bedroom door opened. Two men in overalls came in. They picked me up and placed me on the windowsill and wrapped the sewing machine in an old eiderdown. Next, they dismantled the bed and wrapped it up in big sheets of strong brown paper and string. The curtains and the rug were folded and put into a cardboard carton. Then it was all carried outside and stacked on the path beside the kitchen table and chairs, the sofa, the console radio, the beds from the other bedrooms and the dreaded Trunk, ready to be taken down the hill and put in a goods van on the train. The family was moving. The boys' father had a new job in Invercargill.

I sat alone in the spare bedroom. I listened to the hurried farewells as the boys and their mum and dad said goodbye to the Kariannis family. Just as they were about to close the front door, Frankie Gibbs and Mum O'Donnell came across the back paddock. Mum O had a brown paper bag in one hand. She gave the boys' mum a kiss and said, 'Here's some baking for the train.'

Frankie shook Boy's hand. 'Might see you in Invergiggle sometime.'

With a lot more 'Hurry up, you'll miss the train' and 'Goodbye, don't be a stranger', the family and friends filed down the veranda steps. The front door closed with a bang and the key turned in the lock with a sharp click. Silence.

I was alone in the empty house.

So was this it? The end? I had been rescued from The Trunk only to be left behind without a family to belong to? Would I never see Boy and BB again? Had they really forgotten me?

The afternoon sun reached the bedroom window. My tattered fur and mended body wrapped in the old blanket stood out sharply in the bright golden light. I could understand why they wouldn't find me interesting anymore. My eyes didn't match. My ears were flattened. My paws were patched and my legs had been stitched back on with three different-coloured lengths of wool. I was a wreck, an old toy, something to be thrown away. But they had made me that way. The boys had done this to me! Couldn't they see I was still a young and handsome bear with sparkling eyes on the inside? The crown in the night sky had told me that.

In the distance I could hear the long drawn-out moan of the train whistle. The 2.30 for Invercargill was about to leave.

Tiny noises filled the house. A tap dripped in the kitchen. The wire from the radio aerial slapped against the outside wall of the living room in the breeze. The lock in the front door clicked. *The lock in the front door clicked?!* I heard the door swing open and bang against the doorstop. Footsteps came hurrying down the hall, and the boys' mother appeared in the doorway. She scooped me up and ran out of the house, down the path, through the gate, along the tracks to the train impatiently hissing and puffing steam at the railway station platform.

She climbed up the steep steps into the carriage and found her seat next to her husband.

'Mamma would never have forgiven us if we left old Teddy One-eye behind,' she said, slightly out of breath, as she squeezed me into the luggage rack between two suitcases.

The two boys looked at one another. They said nothing.

The train picked up speed as it rattled past the smattering of houses and cribs along the railway line. The sun, lower now, threw the shadow of the train across the matagouri flats. The carriages were a long, bustling snake. The smoke from the engine, a tall, dark plume of ostrich feathers billowing from the top of a sultan's caravansary.

It was dark when the journey ended. I was carried into the new house, placed in an old brown suitcase with some drawings by Boy and BB, and slid into the top of a wardrobe.

And there I stayed. For seventeen years. Out of sight, forgotten, asleep, hibernating like a flesh-and-blood bear, sometimes dreaming, sometimes remembering, but mainly sleeping.

19
THE WARDROBE YEARS
1955-1972

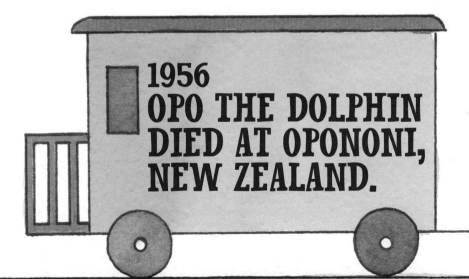

1956
OPO THE DOLPHIN
DIED AT OPONONI,
NEW ZEALAND.

1957
'LET ME BE YOUR TEDDY BEAR' WAS A NO. 1 HIT FOR ELVIS PRESLEY.

1958
THE FIRST NEW ZEALAND SUPERMARKET WAS OPENED IN AUCKLAND.

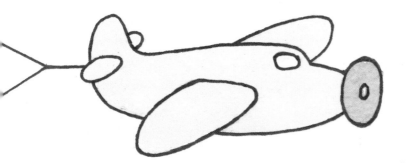

1959
BOY STARTED SECONDARY
SCHOOL IN INVERCARGILL.

1960
TELEVISION BEGAN IN
NEW ZEALAND — TWO
HOURS A NIGHT FOR TWO
NIGHTS A WEEK.

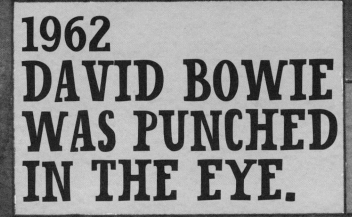

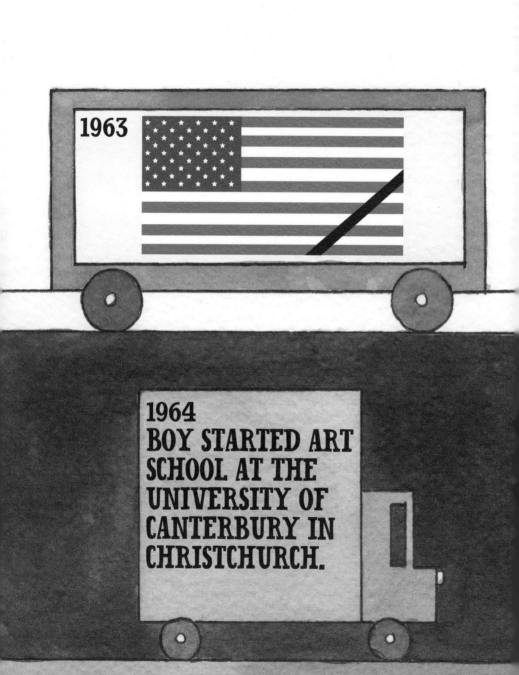

1963

1964
BOY STARTED ART
SCHOOL AT THE
UNIVERSITY OF
CANTERBURY IN
CHRISTCHURCH.

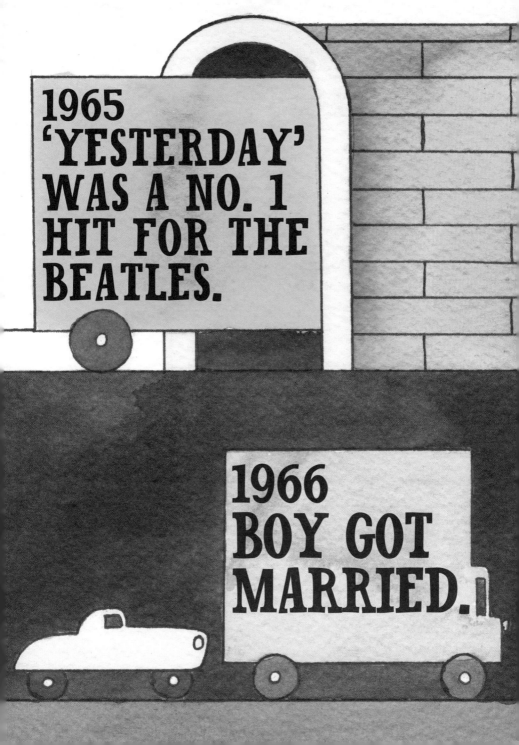

1967

ZZZZZZZZZ
ZZZZZZZZZZZZZ
ZZZZZZZZZZZ...

20
ON THE MOVE AGAIN

THEN, JUST LIKE THAT, without any warning, my suit-case was lifted out of the wardrobe and the lid was opened. Light poured into my black world. I swam up to the surface of the deep pool of sleep and was blinded. Gradually my glass eye adjusted to the brightness, but my button eye was a blur. I recognised Boy's mother as she leaned over the suitcase and packed a wooden buzzy bee, a knitted black and white cat, and a book of nursery rhymes into the gaps around me. She closed the lid, and I fell against the new toys as the suitcase was lifted and carried out of the room.

I was off. Off to somewhere new. This time the journey was by bus and car. At the other end, the suitcase was opened and Boy peered in. But he was no longer a boy. He was a man, a husband and a new father. He laughed when he saw me. 'Old Teddy One-eye,' he said. 'I should tell BB about this.' I was excited. But he picked up the buzzy bee, the knitted cat and the book of nursery rhymes. He lifted them out of the suitcase and closed the lid. He had laughed because I was a joke. His mother had sent me to him as a joke. Had they forgotten that their grandmother told them I was special and should be looked after? Had they not seen the crown in the sky hanging over my head at night, saying I was made for greater things?

The boy pushed the suitcase into the bottom of yet another wardrobe. A wardrobe in the baby's room.

There was no chance of sleeping now. My hibernation had come to an end. If I managed to doze off, the baby would cry to be fed or to be changed or to be picked up. The baby grew. It slept longer at night but it was an early riser.

The baby became a little girl. But then she was joined

by another baby. More crying for food, more crying to be changed or picked up. And just when things began to quieten down, a third baby arrived.

Now there were one, two, three little girls. Three little girls to play with me? To take me on an adventure? The kind of adventure that filled me with fur-tingling excitement and teeth-chattering fear? One that would make me feel alive again? In anticipation, I was once more riding out the bumps in Boy's wheelbarrow and thrilling to a wild escapade in the back of his trike. Yes, I was ready for an adventure with some new children — but these little girls didn't know I existed.

Then, one rainy afternoon, while rummaging in the wardrobe for a blanket to make a hut, the oldest girl found my suitcase. She dragged it out and opened it. To my delight the girl picked me up and hugged me. Later when she'd made the hut at the end of her bed, she invited me to afternoon tea. She had a biscuit covered with hundreds and thousands. She broke a little piece off and poked it into my mouth — or where my mouth would have been if it hadn't been unravelled by her father when he was a boy. She did not seem to mind that my body was a battlefield and my eyes didn't match. She even introduced me to her little sisters when they woke from their afternoon naps.

That night I was lifted into her bed and the next day I was taken in the car to meet her nanna, her mum's mum. Only my head poked out of the old cot blanket that I had been wrapped in all those years before. A big safety pin held it closed. There was no fur left on my face and my ears were about to come off. The girl's grandmother did some running repairs with some thick grey wool.

'Sorry about the colour,' she said. 'But his ears won't come off now.'

21
NEW LIFE, AGAIN
1979

I NO LONGER LIVED in a suitcase at the bottom of a wardrobe. I was part of a family again. The three little girls who had adopted me lived with their mum and dad, twenty-six dolls, 547 books and five goldfish. Their house on a hill looked over Christchurch to the Southern Alps and to the sea. The old cot blanket I had been wrapped in for over twenty years had been put into the wood-burner. My darned and stitched body was squeezed into a floral doll's dress. Baby's booties disguised my patched feet. And although my button eye had not been replaced and my flattened ears were hidden by a bonnet tied under my chin, I could still hear and see everything that was going on.

The girls' dad, Boy, told the girls my name was Teddy One-eye. I was a boy, a man, a he-bear. But the girls wanted a teddy bear that was a girl. They called me Mrs Teddy. So here I was, on the outside a she-bear with a new life and one glass eye, and on the inside a he-bear with a past life.

I had nothing to complain about, though. Being a girl teddy bear was a small price to pay for the fun I now had. The girls invited me to their tea parties. The other dolls were friendly and chatty, especially the Cabbage Patch Kids. They looked upon me as an elderly aunt who had seen the world. And I got out and about. My days of being tossed into a wheelbarrow or in the tray of a trike were over, but the adventures I had with the three little girls, although quieter and less fearful, were lots of fun. The middle-sized girl had a little backpack for me to ride in, and from high on her back I surveyed the world as if from a crow's nest. Sometimes her hair blew into my face. It would have tickled my nose if it hadn't been lying at the bottom of Lake Wakatipu. When she played at a neighbour's house or took her trike for a ride in the garden, she took me with her. At times the excitement of making a hut or building a castle in the sandpit made the girl forget about me. So there were often hurried searches under the hedge or by the fishpond to find me at bedtime.

At the end of the August holidays it was time for the middle girl to start school. Would she take me with her? I wondered. I watched on the morning of her first day as she got out of bed. She stuffed her nightdress under her pillow, pulled on her new school pinafore and laced up her new school shoes. She ran to the kitchen and came back with her new Womble lunchbox already filled with peanut-butter sandwiches and put it her new school bag. She was ready to go to school.

'You woke me up! It is only six o'clock!' growled her older sister. She called to her mother, 'Mum, she's awake already!'

Her mother came into the room and saw the middle girl sitting on her bed, already dressed.

'I told you not to get up so early. It's only 5.30!'

'Actually it's six o'clock, Mum. Your watch. It's old, remember?'

'Well, it's still too early. You'll be tired before you get to school,' said her mother. 'But now you're up, you'd better come and have some porridge. You can't go to school on an empty stomach.'

After breakfast the girls helped their dad hang out some washing, then they lay on the floor drawing until it was 8.30 — finally time to leave for school. Boy, their dad, had already gone to his studio.

'Teeth! Hair! Jackets!' called their mum from the kitchen.

Two minutes later, the middle girl appeared in the doorway. Her school bag hung from one hand, and her backpack with me in it was in the other.

'You can't carry Mrs Teddy as well as your school bag,' said her mother. 'She'll be too heavy for you.'

The girl said nothing. With much struggling she pulled on the backpack, then flipped the school bag over her head so that it hung just behind my back. The girl smiled and slightly raised her eyebrows.

'Hurry up, we'll be late!' shouted her big sister.

The girl followed her out the front door to the footpath that would take them up the hill to school.

'Are you sure you don't want me to come with you?' called their mother.

'No,' replied the younger girl. 'I've got heaps of friends at school.'

'Well, I'll pick you up at two o'clock. Wait by the gate.'

'I hope she doesn't go by her old watch,' said the older girl quietly.

The New Entrants room echoed with squeals and shouts. It sounded like a sty full of excited piglets. Miss Fallows showed the new children where the toilets were and where they could hang their jackets and bags. I was hung on top of the girl's bag, which meant I was able to see through a high window into the classroom. Miss Fallows introduced the new children to the rest of the class. Then she wrote their names on strips of paper and placed them in front of each child. With crayons from a big cardboard box in the art cupboard the new children made drawings of themselves beside their names. This took until morning break.

The children pushed into the cloakroom and grabbed some playlunch to eat outside on the steps. The girl lifted me out of the backpack and took me with her.

A new girl sitting next to her said how much she liked my bonnet and dress. I blushed deeply down inside.

'What's her name?'

'Mrs Teddy, but my dad sometimes calls her Teddy One-eye.'

'Teddy One-eye!' shouted a big boy who was hanging around nearby. 'Teddy One-eye, Teddy One-eye! What a stupid name!'

'Yes, but we don't call her that,' said the girl.

'Hey everyone, did you hear this teddy's name?' called the boy. 'It's Teddy One-eye!'

Other children gathered around. Some laughed, but others sat beside the girl and told her not to take any notice.

At the end of break the girl put me back into the backpack on her coat hook and tucked her jacket over my head. At lunch time she left me there and took only her lunchbox outside. I could no longer see into the classroom, but during the afternoon I heard the children singing as Miss Fallows played the piano. She read stories and poems from School Journals until it was time for the children who had started that day to go home.

At two o'clock the girl slipped my backpack onto her back. She left her jacket tucked tightly around my head to walk across the playground. On top she slung her school bag with her empty lunchbox and her first reading book inside.

At the gate, a group of mums, dads and grandparents stood waiting to walk their children home. The girl took the jacket off my head. With my glass eye I looked to see if I could find her mum. She hadn't arrived, so we sat on the grass inside the gate to wait for her. Her antique watch was often slow. We had all got used to it, so we weren't worried — we knew she would turn up sooner or later. But by ten minutes past two all the new entrants had gone home and we were alone. And that's when we heard it, a sad kind of whimpering, a crying. It was coming from the other side of the school fence.

The girl jumped up and peered through the railings. At the side of the road was a bus stop, and tied to the wooden seat was a small cocker spaniel. Someone had left him there and he was very unhappy.

'Elvis, is that you?' cried the girl. 'What are you doing there?'

The dog stopped crying and looked around. When he saw the girl, his face beamed.

'Woof!' he barked. 'Woofa, woof, woof!'

'Where's your mother? Um, Mrs Partridge, I mean.'

'Woofa, woof!'

'Has she forgotten you again?'

Mrs Partridge was well known all over the hill for her forgetfulness. She was either driving into town and then coming home by bus, or going for a walk and leaving her dog somewhere.

'Well, you can't stay here. I'll take you home.'

I didn't think that was a good idea.

'Mrs Partridge will find Elvis! You don't need to worry,' I shouted silently. But the girl liked adventures as much as

I did, and she saw the chance to have a quick adventure with a little bit of excitement and fear before her mother turned up. Mrs Partridge lived only two doors away from the school, and the girl and her family had been to her house many times. She was sure she could take the dog home and be back again before her mum arrived.

With my backpack and her school bag bobbing on her back, she ran out to the bus stop and untied the dog. Elvis jumped to lick her face but the girl ducked. I was not pleased when his tongue slid across the back of my head and left a trail of spit. It reminded me of my adventures with Black Nin in Kingston when Boy was a boy.

'Woofa, woof!' The dog tried to run ahead when we turned into Mrs Partridge's gate. He led us up the drive lined with daffodils to the front door. The girl sprang up the red steps and rang the bell. She waited and rang again. There was no reply. The girl came back down the steps and walked further down the drive, past even more daffodils, to a gate at the side of the house that let us into the back yard. The girl knocked on the back door. Again no one answered.

'Your mum will be at the school gate by now,' I tried to remind the girl. And, as if she heard me, she tied the dog to the rotary clothesline. She found his water bowl at the edge of the lawn and filled it from a hose attached to the back of the garage. The girl searched her lunchbox for something for the dog to eat, but there were only crumbs in the lunch paper and a brown apple core. Elvis sniffed the core and went back his water bowl. There was nothing more we could do for the dog. He was home again, he had something to drink and we were sure his owner would be back soon.

So we started to walk towards the gate. But Elvis didn't like that. He didn't want to be on his own. He started howling and barking and crying so loudly that the girl turned back and untied his leash and led him to the back porch. The three of us sat down on the step. The dog was happy but we wanted to leave.

After a few minutes, the girl stood up. But Elvis set up such a terrible woofing we had to sit down again. He stopped yelping immediately and smiled a big doggy smile.

By now the girl's mother would be waiting at the school gate, but there was no way of telling her where we were. The dog was quiet and settled. 'Let's leave him,' I suggested quietly. He was behaving like a spoilt child. But the girl could not do it. She felt sorry for Elvis. She had known him a long time and had often taken him for walks. He was her friend. She would keep him company until Mrs Partridge got home. There was nothing else she could do.

The afternoon shadows stretched across the back lawn. And it got colder. We should have been home by now. The girl put her jacket on, and the three of us huddled together to keep warm in the back porch.

The sun had slipped down behind the garage when we heard a car coming up the drive. Elvis ran to the gate. Mrs Partridge opened it and came into the back yard.

'Elvis, have you been a good boy?' Then she noticed us. 'Hello, dear. Did you pick him up from the dog groomer's? I went to pick him up but he wasn't there.'

'No,' said the girl. 'I found him at the bus stop.'

'Oh, you naughty boy. Were you trying to catch the bus and run away?'

'He was crying so I brought him home.'

'Did I leave him there?' asked Mrs Partridge.

The girl said nothing.

'Perhaps I did,' said the woman. 'I thought I took him to have a haircut. But I must have left him by the bus stop this morning when I took him for a walk. I am getting forgetful.'

That's nothing new, I thought to myself.

'But you should be getting home, dear. You'll miss your

dinner. Come on, I'll give you a ride.'

When we arrived at the girl's house, her mum and dad were coming down the street from different directions. They had been searching the neighbourhood and asking people if they had seen their daughter. A police car was parked outside the house. I could hear the crackle of a radio through its open window.

The three of us scrambled out of Mrs Partridge's car — Elvis first, followed by the girl and me. Boy ran and picked his daughter up and held her tightly. Her mum gave them both a big hug. Then the girl burst into tears. 'I'm busting,' she said. 'I want to do wees, badly!'

While the two eldest girls were at school the next day, their mother took their little sister and me to town. At the top of her shopping list was a new watch.

22
FAMILY SECRETS
1982

SUMMER HOLIDAYS THIS YEAR were to be down south. A week after the longest day had been and gone, and the Christmas tree had been stripped of decorations and taken to the tip, the family packed the car. With airbeds and sleeping bags tied to the roof, and the boot crammed with summer clothes and food, we set off down the main south road.

I sat on a beach ball in the back seat between the two

youngest girls. My glass eye followed the smooth flat plains of Canterbury as they flowed along both sides of the car and out towards the mountains. My button eye tried to count the number of bridges we had to cross to get over the wide braided rivers. And my ears listened to the songs and stories that the tape deck played to keep the girls from squabbling. It was a quiet journey, though. And it blew away the cobwebs more gently than the trip I took with Boy and his family that Sunday in Kingston many years before.

Riverton, on the coast near Invercargill, was the destination. Like Kingston, Riverton had taken on legendary proportions in the stories of Boy's family. During the wardrobe years, Boys' grandmother had died, and so had his mum and dad. His parents had been buried up north, but his grandmother had been taken back to Riverton to lie beside her husband.

So Riverton it was this year. A two-day trip from Christchurch, with a stop for a night at a motel in Dunedin. The girls' dad said that this holiday would be a chance for them to get to know the salty little town where many of their ancestors had lived. It would be a chance, too, to visit the grave of Boy's grandmother, their great-grandmother. I wanted to visit it too. I missed her.

She was the only person who saw my true worth. She took care of me, stood up for me and mended my wounds when playtime got rough.

The little holiday house on the outskirts of town, not far from the cemetery, was surrounded by paddocks of long grass edged with macrocarpa shelterbelts that hadn't been trimmed in years. As soon as their father pulled up outside the low blue weatherboard cottage, the girls climbed out of the back seat and raced off across the paddocks to explore. The ants in their pants wouldn't let them sit still any longer. It had been a long time, crammed into the back seat with pillows, books, toys and crumbs. I didn't mind either, when I was picked up and stuffed into my backpack. I didn't want to be left behind to watch the unpacking of the car.

I swung from side to side in the backpack, my glass eye snatching glimpses of the long black arms of the trees scratching the afternoon sky. My button eye looked down into the lush green grass splashed with cowpats.

At the far side of the biggest paddock, at the end of a row of macrocarpa, stood a hawthorn tree. Its branches swooped down to touch the ground, polishing the earth smooth as marble, clearing it of any vegetation. Buried within its tangled limbs were the fragments of a picket fence and a gate that had been pushed forward by a large branch. Two thick gateposts stood on either side, still upright, with a crushed letterbox.

The girls stopped in front of the hawthorn tree. I strained to see what they were looking at. Gradually, through the branches, I made it out — an unpainted wooden house with a rusted tin roof. Brick chimneys sat alert, like rabbit's ears, and the long arms of two wild flower beds reached out to us as they stretched towards the gate. Directly in front of the house stood giant rose bushes bent under the weight of their blooms, and willowy foxgloves and granny's bonnets ran all over the paths like wayward children. The front door was flanked by two windows that looked like eyes.

The house had a sad face, and it was one I knew. I had seen it before. Why was this place so familiar? A tattered memory fluttered forward in my mind like a moth at a misty window.

'Okay, I'm going to have a look,' said the middle girl. She moved towards the tree. I went with her because I was on her back. I had no choice. Excitement and fear. I could smell an adventure.

Reluctantly, not wanting to miss out, the oldest and the youngest girls followed.

It became quiet as we crept under the low branches of the hawthorn tree and scrambled into the garden. No birds sang. No crickets screeked. The granny's bonnets flowing around the girls' feet were turned to gold by afternoon sunlight coming through the gaps under the wall of macrocarpa that blocked the view of the house from the holiday crib.

The house stood still. Not that I expected it to move, but it looked as if it was holding its breath. It was guarded and wary. Playing possum.

'Come on,' said the middle girl. 'Let's explore.'

The oldest girl didn't move. 'I reckon that house is looking at us,' she said. She had always been told that her imagination got the better of her. Just like her dad when he was little. I thought of the beast at the dairy near his grandmother's house in Invercargill.

But this time she was right. She could feel it, and so could I: this old place was definitely watching us with its high black window-eyes, following our every move. And I was sure it could smell us, was straining to catch our scent with its gaping door-nose like a ferret after a rabbit. Above all else, though, I knew it was taking particular notice of me.

'Why is it so quiet?' whispered the little girl.

The middle girl shrugged. 'Dunno.' She made off towards the house. On her back, I sailed like a galleon over the lemon and violet sea of wildflowers towards the broken wooden steps that led up to the veranda.

Something moved across the window in front of us. The reflection of a cloud? A bird? An eyeball? Did the house just sigh? I listened hard. Nothing.

The girl (and I) stepped onto the parched boards of the veranda. They groaned slightly under our weight. Nails, torn loose by years of rain and sun, hung down like ragged teeth from the planks that had sprung free.

The girl hesitated, but her sisters were right behind her. They tumbled up the steps and banged into her back. I could have fallen out of my backpack. Luckily, the girl had my pack fastened tightly around her waist, so I stayed firmly in place. I didn't want to be left there if the girls suddenly decided to flee and run home.

Clutching each other, the sisters found the nerve to edge towards the yawning entrance. The door had slumped against the wall of the hall. Its handle had gouged a hole in the striped wallpaper, exposing layers of previous papers glued over the scrim. Halfway down the hall was a small table covered with plaster dust from where the ceiling mouldings had become damp and fallen down. A carpet runner ran from the doorway off into the belly of the house and disappeared into the gloom. Where the rain had blown in, tiny toadstools and elderberry seedlings grew in the carpet pile, creating a 3-D version of the woven floral pattern beneath.

Moving as one, we stepped over the doorstep. Toadstools were crushed underfoot and prints appeared in the thick dust and dirt on the floorboards.

To the right was a bedroom. The door was ajar. We looked in. A double bed with a mouldy eiderdown stood with its head against the far wall. A rag mat partly covered the wooden floor, and torn lace curtains hung in shreds over the dark green blind that had been pulled down to cover the window. Dust fairies danced in the sabres of afternoon sunlight that slipped through slits in the blind and created brilliant patches of light on the dark, floral wallpaper covering the walls and ceiling.

Dogs, cats, birds, rats, mice and beetles had all made this room their home from time to time. Bones, skeletons, sticks, straw, mud and droppings covered every surface. And lying over the top of this debris I could sense a thick, invisible quilt of sadness stitched by the hand of a broken heart.

'Ooh, what a dump!' said the middle girl.

I agreed.

'Whoever left this place did so in a big hurry. They didn't even bother to take their furniture,' said the big girl.

'Or their clothes,' said the little girl who had boldly gone into the room and opened the door of the wardrobe.

This made the rest of us feel quite brave. We crossed the dirty floor and stood behind the little girl. The wardrobe door squeaked as it swung shut. We stared at our shattered images in its broken mirror. Three little girls and a bear dressed as a girl, standing in a jigsaw bedroom waiting to be put together to complete a puzzle.

In a corner of the jagged picture I noticed a framed photograph hanging on the wall by the bed. A little boy sat on his mother's knee. Propped up beside him was a teddy bear.

I wanted to look closer, but the girls moved from the wardrobe to explore the rest of the room. On the far side of the bed was a cane cot. Convolvulus had climbed up through a broken floorboard and filled the space in the tiny bed where a baby had once slept. Behind the cot was a chest of drawers, the top and sides streaked by birds.

The middle girl leaned forward and yanked the top drawer open. I looked over her shoulder at the newspaper cuttings, letters and cards inside. As she rummaged through the papers, I saw cards and letters with the word 'sympathy' in large letters. She unfolded a sheet of aged newspaper. I managed to read most of it before she pushed the drawer closed.

RARE DIPHTHERIA CASES STRIKE THE SOUTH

(P.A.)   INVERCARGILL, July 12, 1940

A rare outbreak of diphtheria has been reported in Southland with two cases in Winton and Riverton. The Superintendent of Southland Hospital said "that health services had been taken completely by surprise."

It became clear. The baby whose bed was now filled with vines had died. He was the boy in the picture on the wall. The boy with the teddy bear. The teddy with the . . .

'Sparkly eyes! This bear's got sparkly eyes!' shouted the littlest girl, who was now standing in front of the picture I had seen in the mirror. The other girls ran to have a look.

'Look!' she shouted. 'This teddy's got sparkly eyes just like Mrs Teddy!'

'But Mrs Teddy's only got one eye,' said the oldest girl.

'Yeah, but it's sparkly like this teddy's,' said the middle girl.

'He's much newer than our teddy,' said the oldest girl.

'Yeah, I know, 'cause our teddy bear is old! She used to be Dad's,' shouted the little girl, trying to get her point across. 'But look at the eyes! They are exactly like our teddy's eye!'

Even though the photograph was black and white, the eyes of the teddy bear on the wall in this sad house looked the same as my single glass eye made of warm brown glass with flecks of yellow-gold. Was this a photograph of my brother? Was it my father? Or was it a picture of me? Of me in another life?

In my head, the moth once more fluttered against the misty window.

Something started to shape itself. Chips became fragments, fragments became chunks.

Chunks became . . .

I didn't have time to ponder more. From under the pile of rotting bedclothes came a snuffling, grunting sound.

The girls' chatter stopped. They looked at one another.

'Wasn't me,' said the middle girl.

'And it wasn't me,' I said silently.

The sounds came again. Then, from under the bed, a bleary-eyed possum, woken from its afternoon slumber, with claws scratching and sliding on the wooden floorboards, ran towards the girls. At first they thought it was the teddy bear in the photograph. But its plump, furry body looked as if it had been put together by a mad toy maker. And its eyes were not brown with flecks of yellow-gold. They were big and black like two lumps of shiny coal.

The girls screamed and ran. I fell backwards as the middle girl raced through the front door and leapt off the veranda. My backpack, which had been firmly fastened at her waist, became loose. I was about to fall out, but one of my legs got caught in the frame. I was left hanging upside down, swinging violently from one side to the other. The blousy roses and the spiky foxgloves hung out of the sky. As the girls scrambled under the hawthorn tree, my back and arms were caught and torn. My bonnet came loose, and one of my ears was ripped until it was held by only a thread.

'You're just in time to help your mother make the beds,' said their father as the three girls tumbled through the back door of the holiday cottage.

'But Dad,' panted the little girl, 'we saw a ghost!'

'A teddy bear ghost!' shouted the middle girl.

'It was hiding under the bed,' said the oldest girl. 'Waiting for us . . .'

'You and your imagination,' their father said, giving his oldest daughter a hug. 'You've got your sisters seeing things now too.'

'But Dad,' said the little girl again. 'We did see a teddy bear ghost and he—'

'Now,' he said, 'settle down. What have you been doing to old Teddy One-eye? He's only holding on by one leg.'

I was lifted gently out of the backpack. Later that night, my new wounds were stitched and mended. My ear was sewn back on. 'Sorry, I had to use white cotton,' said their mum. 'It's all I could find.'

23
THE MIST CLEARS

THE GIRLS AND I HELPED their mum and dad gather some early mushrooms from the paddock in front of the cottage. In the tiny kitchen, the parents stewed them for breakfast and spooned them onto their plates, turning their toast black like slabs of diseased liquorice. The girls had honey and toast.

'I think we'll go into Riverton this morning. Have a look around,' said the girls' dad. 'We used to come here for a Sunday drive from Invercargill when BB and I were kids.'

The girls' mum came from Christchurch. She didn't know this place at all. Boy was in his element.

'This is where Mamma, your great-grandmother, used to live,' he said as we drove along the coast road into Riverton. 'We'll go and see her grave later if you like.'

'Do we have to?' asked the middle girl.

They parked the car by the museum. I was stuffed into my backpack.

'Mrs Scandret used to live in this street,' said the girls' dad.

Little diamonds of sunlight glinted in the surf on the beach that ran up to the road.

'Can't we go and collect some shells?' asked the little girl.

'Yeah, let's!' said the middle girl.

'We'll go for a short walk first,' said Boy.

I could tell he had something planned.

We made our way up a steep street that offered views of the bay and the Takitimu mountains in the distance. It was new for the girls and their mum, but that moth at the window kept telling me I had been there before.

The houses were small and wooden, painted in bright, clear colours that might have been chosen by children. Yellow walls and pale-pink window frames. Bright blue roofs and red doors. Weekend colours. It was as if the owners believed they would be happier if they were permanently on holiday.

'Mrs Scandret's place! This is it!'

'Who's Mrs Scandret?' asked the girls' mother.

'I wonder if she's home?' said the girls' dad without answering the question.

He opened the small mauve corrugated-iron gate, and walked down the path lined with giant scallop shells. We followed behind. In front of us sat a small house, painted mauve to match the gate. Paua shells plastered to the frame above the front door caught the light and threw it around the shallow porch. Two old boots filled with plastic daisies sat either side of the front steps.

Boy knocked on a pane of bubble-glass in the door.

It opened quickly, as if the elderly woman drying her hands on her apron was expecting them. 'Hello,' she said, smiling. 'Have you come to see me?'

'Mrs Scandret?'

'That's right.'

'Mrs Scandret, my grandmother's friend?'

'Granny MacKay?' asked the woman. 'I thought you had a MacKay look about you.'

She came through the door and gave Boy a hug.

'This is my family,' he said.

'Well, well. This is a nice surprise. Come on in. Make yourselves at home.'

We followed Mrs Scandret inside. She led us to her good front room and went in first to switch on the electric heater with artificial coals. The room was musty and cold.

The view of the bay and distant mountains was obscured by drapes, a venetian blind and scalloped net curtains. A small watercolour painting of the same scene hung on the wall above the electric fire.

Boy introduced everyone. Last of all he said, 'And you probably remember Teddy, Teddy One-eye?'

The girls looked at their father. They didn't like that name.

'Your teddy bear!' said Mrs Scandret. 'Your grandmother used to talk about him often. You boys were pretty rough on him, though. It used to upset your grandmother when you didn't take better care of him.'

Boy went red.

'But we still have him. The girls play with him now.'

'Let me see him.'

The middle girl took the backpack off and lifted me out.

'That's a pretty frock he's wearing,' said the old lady.

I was embarrassed. Couldn't those girls see I was a boy-bear?

'She needs that dress to keep her together,' said the oldest girl.

'Yeah, she's falling apart,' added the little girl.

'I see he — I mean she — still has the button eye your granny gave him.'

'How do you know about that?' asked Boy.

'You swallowed the real one,' said Mrs Scandret.

Once again, Boy blushed brighter than the electric coal fire.

'Granny MacKay had a button tin,' she said. 'She let me look through it whenever she babysat me. She took it everywhere with her, just in case.'

'I remember it too,' said Boy.

Mrs Scandret left the room and returned with a small biscuit tin with a sailing ship embossed on the lid. She placed it on a small table near Boy.

'Your granny gave me this not long before she died. She knew I had always liked it.' She opened the lid. Buttons, plain and fancy, black, brown, maroon, green, red and clear, glistened like the jewels in a pirate's treasure chest.

'Here's another one just like Teddy's.' Mrs Scandret picked up a small black button and held it up to my button eye. 'That was a lovely jacket. When she had finished with it, your grandmother kept the buttons to remind her of it.'

'Can I have a look, please?' asked the middle girl.

'Yes, dear, of course you can.'

I watched as the girl plunged her hands into buttons and let them fall through her fingers like Scrooge McDuck enjoying his money.

'Look, there's some paper here. Is it a letter?'

She handed it to Mrs Scandret.

'Funny, I've never noticed it before.' She unfolded the paper and began to read silently. She stopped and said, 'Listen to this:

Dundee House
Riverton
11th December 1940

Dear Granny Mac,

It is with an extremely heavy heart that I write on the eve of our departure for Scotland. We can no longer stay here in a country where we lost our darling wee Jamie to that unforgiving disease.

Angus and I will leave in only the clothes we stand up in. We fear the belongings we had here might, if taken back to our home in Dumfries, forever remind us of the sorrowful time we had in Riverton.

As a mark of our deep affection and to say thank you for your support, we would like you to go to our house after we have gone and take something of Jamie's that will remind you of the time you spent with him.

Farewell and God bless,
Your affectionate friend,

Ruth Kincaid.

Mrs Scandret slowly folded the letter in two.

'Just a minute,' she said. 'There's a note on the back in pencil. It says:

I collected the teddy bear still in its box.
I will keep him for someone special.

M. MacKay Jan. 1941.

'I remember Granny MacKay telling me about that dear
wee boy.' Mrs Scandret clasped the letter to her chest with
both hands. She looked up into the face of Boy. 'She spent
a lot of time sitting with Jamie when he was sick, right
until the end. She loved him very much. That is obviously
why she took something really special like his teddy bear
and gave him to you.'

I watched as Boy and his family became as pale and still
as a group of plaster casts. The room was silent except for
the whirring of the fan in the electric coal fire. Boy's eyes
were sparkling, wet. He blinked a couple of times and bent
forward to listen to something the littlest girl whispered to
him. She wanted a drink of water.

Mrs Scandret moved too. She put the letter back in the
button tin and closed the lid.

'That's a gloomy old subject. It's too nice a day for that.
Let's all have a nice cup of tea. Would you girls like some
lemonade?'

My glass eye sparkled brighter that it had ever done before. In my mind, the moth sat still. The window was no longer misty. I could see right through it, back into the past. I hadn't been a new bear when I was given to Boy after all. I had been part of another child's life. And I could now remember that boy clearly. He was Jamie, my little Jamie.

24
TWO BOXES
1940

THE SOUND OF WEEPING in the cold house was echoed by the sigh of the sea somewhere off in the dark. My best friend, little Jamie, had died.

When he was born, he was as pale as a twig that had never seen the sun. As he grew from a fragile baby into a sickly boy, we were always together. He had a little wicker chair to sit on beside the big sofa in the living room, and I had mine. At the long wooden table in the kitchen, my high chair sat next to his. Both chairs were painted sky blue to match. At bedtime Jamie got into bed first to lie next to the wall. Then he lifted me into place along the outside edge. He knew I would protect him from the monsters that might rush through the door or sneak from under the bed when the light went out. I was his guardian and his friend, and he loved me. And even though life was quiet and uneventful, I did not mind. I didn't know about adventures full of excitement and fear.

Because Jamie got tired easily, we spent most of our days indoors. There were rare times on warm days when his mum or dad carried him out to the bench made of twisted manuka branches on the sheltered side of the house. Propped up against a stack of pillows, as the westerly sprung off the roof and roared overhead, we watched the butterflies in the buddleia or the bees in the foxgloves just long enough to get a little colour in his cheeks. Back inside, he brushed my fur and polished my glass eyes with his sleeve.

Some nights, if the blinds on his bedroom window were left up, the light from the Southern Cross would reflect in my eyes. Little Jamie would say, 'I can see some diamonds. Hold still, I'll catch them and make a crown for your head.'

I never left his side as Jamie grew older and a little

stronger. During the day, I listened as he recited his times tables with Ruth, his mother, or watched as he played pick-up-sticks on the mat in front of the fire.

And every night without fail I lay like the Great Wall of China along the edge of his bed to protect him from the monsters and the goblins. And, except for an occasional nightmare, I managed to keep those creatures at bay.

But the diphtheria goblins were cunning. They made themselves invisible, and one night with the sky leaking like a rusted cauldron they slid silently under the door, right before my ever-watchful eyes. From their slimy sacks they sprinkled seeds of sickness over Jamie's chest. As he slept, he sucked them down into his lungs where they germinated and set root, spreading their twisting tendrils throughout his body.

That winter, when Jamie became ill, his mother hovered angel-like above his bed, seeing to his every need. My sparkly eyes watched her hold his hand and stroke his forehead, or gently lift a spoon to his mouth with some thin soup or warm milk. Jamie's father would call the cows in early to hurry through the milking so he could go to his boy's bedside too.

The westerlies brought the rain every afternoon. And when they were calm, cold rain came from the south.

The people in the farms and cottages sprinkled across the green hills edging the sea were aware of the family's plight. A pot of soup, a basket of scones or a large mutton pie were often left at the kitchen door. Others offered to help with cleaning or washing and ironing, but they were kindly thanked and sent away. Only one person was welcomed in. Granny MacKay would bike out from the town and, after hanging up her sodden scarf and coat by the coal range, slip quietly into Jamie's bedroom. She would wave the boy's parents off to bed, settle into a chair in the shadows by the door and turn up the night-light so she could see her crocheting. If I had fallen out of Jamie's bed, she tucked me back in. And there she stayed until Ruth came back from a few hours of sleep to bring the old lady a cup of tea.

The doctor came every day. His car skidded on the muddy drive up to the gate by the hawthorn tree in front of the house. Some days he had to give up and walk to check on his tiny patient, leaving the old Holden slouched against the black forest of flax. But the doctor could do little to stop the growth of the goblins' evil forest filling every corner of Jamie's body with its twisted branches, its thorns and its dark greasy flowers.

And now Jamie's tiny, wasted body, dressed in a white

nightshirt, lay in a white coffin lined with pale-blue satin. The box had been placed on his bed. His fingers were interwoven on his chest and his blond hair was brushed forward to soften the gauntness of his face.

His mother stood hunched like a small black bird. Her hands, trembling in front of her stomach, were woven like her son's. A brooch of three entwined hearts glowed with a dull sheen at her throat, and the winter roses on the bedside table shook with her sobs. She pulled her fingers apart and bent forward. From under the boy's bed, she pulled out a cardboard box. It was the one from the toy shop, with the Southern Cross on the lid, the one I came in. She slid it onto the bed next to her little boy's coffin. She took off the lid and put me inside.

For two days we lay there, little Jamie in his box, me in mine. Neighbours came with flowers, cards and tears, and sometimes things to eat. And day and night Ruth, the boy's mother, sat by the bed and wept.

On the third day it was time for the little boy to take his last journey down the muddy drive and along the road with the sea lashing the rocks to the little church by the cemetery near the racecourse. Two men in sombre coats and pinstriped trousers came, heads bowed, into the boy's bedroom. The boy's mother and father moved back to allow them to do their work. One of the men placed the lid on the boy's box. The boy's parents were holding each other, too distraught to watch. Then he put the lid on my box.

I was plunged into darkness. I felt my box move as someone lifted it. A flood of fear rushed from my feet to my ears. Every hair on my body was standing to attention. My silent scream for help filled my dark prison. I was to be buried with little Jamie. But I was still alive!

Then I heard them — the words of my salvation.

'Not that one, Chas. Just the boy's.'

I felt my box settle back down on the bed. Then I listened as the muffled voices and the sound of weeping got gradually quieter. I relaxed. My arms and legs went limp, my eyes clouded over and I fell into a coma-like sleep. I was so saddened at the death of my friend, I stayed like that for a very long time. Even my rescue by Granny MacKay from the house of sadness did not wake me.

During those long, dark years in the box, fragments of memory or a name drifted through my head without making sense. Like the sleeping princess who could be woken only by someone who would love her, I lay in my cardboard casket, waiting, without knowing it, to be released by a new playmate. I was waiting for another boy or girl to make me their friend — waiting to be reborn.

And when it happened on that winter's afternoon in 1950, I opened my eyes to a new life, the sad memories of little Jamie cemented to the bottom of a deep well somewhere inside my furry chest.

25
THE HOUSE ON THE HILL
1982

ON OUR RETURN FROM RIVERTON, I was taken out of my dress. The booties were given to a baby doll and my bonnet was put into a bag for the Salvation Army. Now that some of my story was known, I was treated with more respect. The untidy patches on my arms and legs remained the same, and so did the white cotton in my ear, but now I was dressed in a smart sailor's suit and allowed to sleep in a little wooden cot with a painted boat at my head and a shell at my feet.

But still I saw little of Boy. He always seemed to be busy writing and drawing. He would brush me aside when the girls suggested he look at my new suit. He barely looked up from his drawing board if someone commented on how smart I looked. I suspected that my battle-scarred body was an embarrassment to him, a reminder of his childhood days. I had been rescued from the house of sorrows and placed in his care. But he had treated me roughly sometimes, and did not always care that his baby brother did the same. I wanted him to see we could be good friends again.

The girls treated me well, but they now looked beyond the toy box for friends and companions. An old teddy bear, even one with a long history, was of little interest to children who were growing up.

So it was off to the back bedroom. Stuff went in there but nothing came out. It was a storage place for jigsaw puzzles with large pieces, junior card games, and dolls with their tiny tea sets in boxes secured with rubber bands. I knew this kind of place well. First there had been The Trunk, then the suitcase in the wardrobes, and now the back bedroom.

My little cot was pushed between a brocade tub chair

with a torn cover and a bookcase. With my glass eye, I scanned the titles on the spines of the books over and over again, and could recite them all in correct order without looking. *Peter Pan, Revolting Rhymes, The Lion in the Meadow, My Cat Likes to Hide in Boxes,* and on and on.

I wondered whatever had happened to *Ruth Fielding and the Gypsies.* My mind wandered back to the brave mother, also called Ruth, who sat for all those weeks beside the bed of her sick boy, my friend little Jamie. Would he have set me aside when he grew up? Would his mother have stored me away in a suitcase at the top of a wardrobe? Would my life have been any different living with them?

With my button eye, I watched a spider across the room build a nest under a Formica table. In the spring, I counted the hundreds of spider babies as they hatched. The leaves on the sycamore I could see through the window above the bookcase burst forth with a green so vibrant it almost hurt my glass eye to look at it. Summer. Autumn. The sycamore leaves turned brown and fell. Winter. Southerly rain beat against the window. I lay in my cot, not completely forgotten but simply overlooked.

26
THE BACK BEDROOM
1986–1996

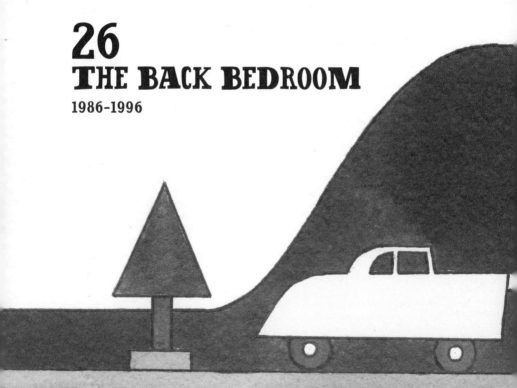

1986
THE FIRST
TEDDY BEAR
MUSEUM WAS
OPENED IN
GERMANY.

1991
A SWEDISH POP GROUP CALLED 'THE TEDDYBEARS' WAS FORMED.

1992
'THE TEDDY BEARS' CHRISTMAS' MOVIE WAS RELEASED.

27
THE JUNK OF AGES
1997

THE DOOR TO THE back bedroom had remained closed for years, then one day it opened and Boy came in.

'Wow, there's a lot of junk in here,' he said, calling over his shoulder to his wife. 'I think we should throw it all out. Make this room into a really nice guest room.'

He walked over to the bookcase and pulled the tub chair away to look at the books. He was obviously surprised to see me lying there in my cot. He must have forgotten that I had been left there years before. Perhaps he never even knew?

He stood still. Not moving. Barely breathing. His mother, his father, his baby brother, Granny MacKay, Frankie Gibbs, Len Hume and all his friends from childhood danced like a procession through his head. Then he blinked a couple of times and reached into the cot. He picked me up and said, 'The rest of this stuff can go to the Sallies, but I had better keep you, old Teddy One-eye. I'd never hear the end of it if I tossed you out.'

Boy carried me out to the kitchen and took a fresh black plastic rubbish bag from the drawer near the stove. He dropped me in, tied the bag at the top, and took it down to the basement where all unwanted things that perhaps shouldn't be thrown away just yet were stored. Boy hung the bag on a nail. He switched off the light and closed the door, leaving me to darkness.

Above the hum of the deep freeze and the clicks and gurgles of the washing machine I listened to footsteps, loud then soft, as they crossed overhead. From the living room above, the television kept me in touch with the rest of the world.

28
THE BASEMENT
1997–2011

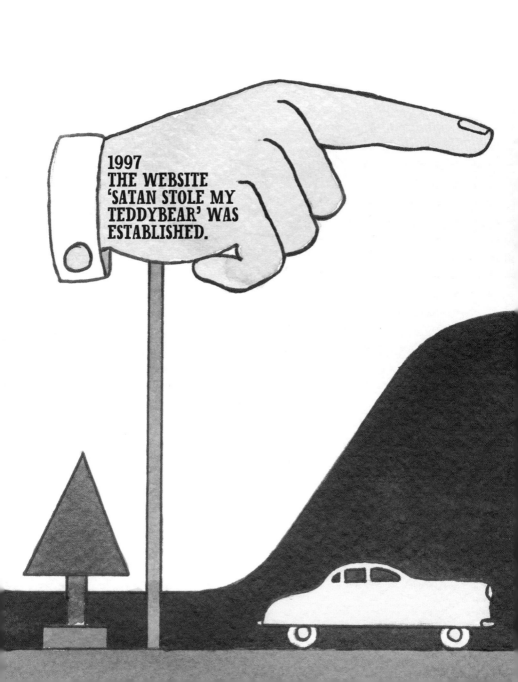

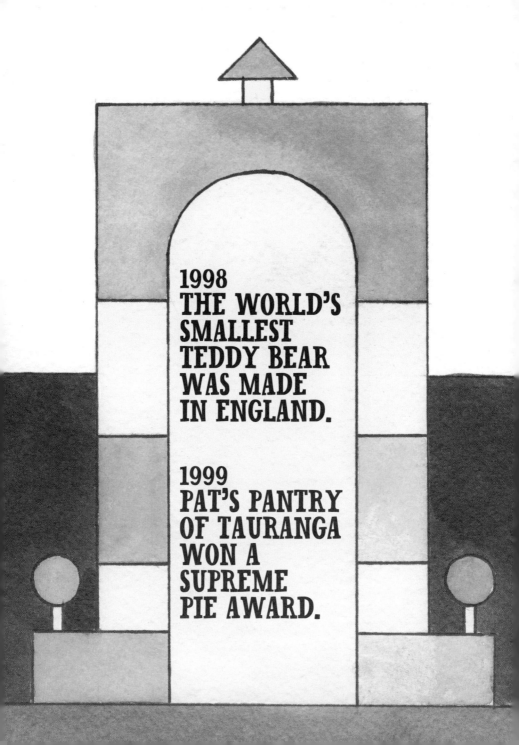

1998
THE WORLD'S SMALLEST TEDDY BEAR WAS MADE IN ENGLAND.

1999
PAT'S PANTRY OF TAURANGA WON A SUPREME PIE AWARD.

2000
BOY'S BOOK 'THE
HOUSE THAT JACK
BUILT' WAS THE
NEW ZEALAND
CHILDREN'S BOOK
OF THE YEAR.

2003
DOLLY THE CLONED SHEEP DIED ON VALENTINE'S DAY.

2004
ZZZZZZZ
ZZZZZZZZ
ZZZZZZZZZ
ZZZZZZ...

2005
ZZZZZZZZZZ
ZZZZZZZZZZZZZzz
ZZZZZZZZzzzz...

2006
ZZZZ
ZZZZZ
ZZZZZZZZ
ZZZZZzzz
zzzz...

2007
800,000 FREE
TEDDY BEARS
WERE RECALLED IN
CANADA BECAUSE ONE
CHILD CHEWED OFF
HER BEAR'S
EYE.

2008
SOOTY BEAR
TURNED 60.

2009 ZZZZZZZZZZZZZ
ZZZZZZZZZZ...

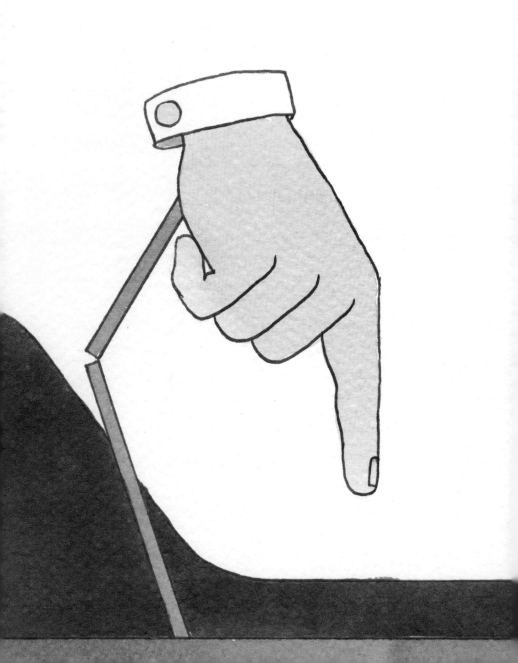

2010–2011 MAJOR EARTH-QUAKES STRIKE CHRISTCHURCH, NEW ZEALAND.

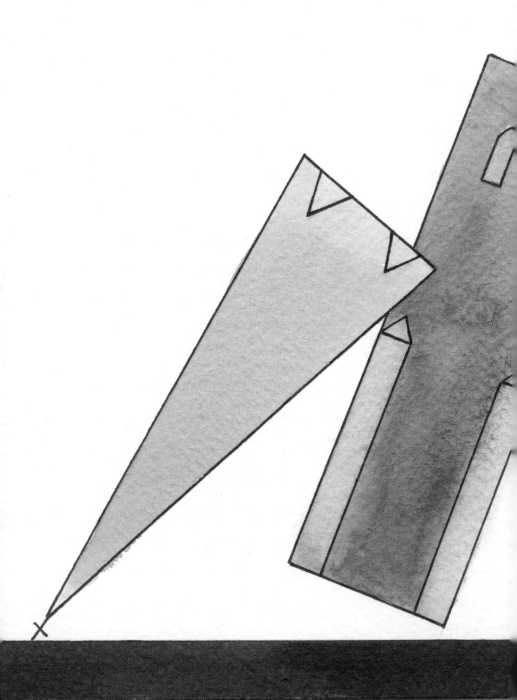

THROUGH A GASH TORN in the rubbish bag by a hungry cat that was trapped in the basement for a week, I watched Boy and his wife do the laundry, add food to the deep freeze, or store away unwanted household items. Mice came out at night and raced along the floor joists. Sometimes a rat would scurry in, looking for a warm spot to nest for the winter. Straw flowers crackled and popped as they hung drying next to my black bag. At Christmas time, the plastic Christmas tree, already dressed, was taken upstairs and brought back again eight days later.

In its own way, the basement offered more life than the spare room. The passing of time shown in the greening and browning of the sycamore had been stopped when the tree was cut down. Even the spider under the table seemed to catch something and die. Its cobweb hung forlornly until it collapsed into tatters, lifting and falling in the slightest movement of air.

When the earthquakes came, my bag swung on its nail, but it didn't fall.

29
TRANSFIGURATION

DURING THE DAY OF THE NIGHT it happened, the quakes had been quiet. No one had visited the basement. Neither man nor mouse. In my solitude, I drifted into a dream where I wandered along the winding corridors of memory. Towering blue glass walls allowed glimpses of children, animals and toys who had been my companions throughout the years. Their stories played like old movies behind the uneven glass. I followed the hallways, twisting and turning, up and down stairs, until I came to a high-ceilinged chamber where two beds stood. Yellow leaves blown by a silent wind rustled across the floor and built up against my legs. I went further into the room. In one bed lay Jamie. Asleep. A boy.

In the other was Boy. Asleep. A man.

My almost hairless body bristled with excitement and fear as I looked down on sleeping Boy, remembering the adventures I had had with him.

I turned to Jamie. A warm cloud of love engulfed me. I was lifted off my feet and embraced by invisible arms. I wallowed in the golden glow, knowing that this was part of the promise made by the crown in the sky. I started to count backwards from ten. Ten, nine, eight, seven, six, five . . .

The basement door opened. I looked out of the hole in the bag, expecting to see Boy or his wife. Although the light by the door had not been switched on, the basement was lit with a soft, milky gleam. Standing in the open door was a small boy in a white shirt that hung to just below his knees, his pale hair forward over his pale forehead. The soft light that fell across the washing machine and the deep freeze was coming from him. He was a lamp, a torch, a light bulb, glowing like the bunny night-light that BB had had when he was afraid of the dark.

I saw the boy coming towards me without moving his legs. His feet together, toes pointing down, floating, coming closer as if I was looking through the zoom lens of a camera. When he reached my black rubbish bag, he lifted his arms and pulled it from the nail. He lowered it to the basement floor and undid the string. The bag fell to my feet. I stood before him. He bent slightly and cupped the back of my head with his hand. I looked up into his smiling face. It was Jamie. My little Jamie! He picked me up and, holding me tightly to his chest, carried me outside.

For a moment we stood on the lawn, breathing in the smell of newly cut grass. A heavy sea fog rolling in from the east had just reached the house, and it was still thin enough in places to allow the full moon to shine through.

The fog grew thicker and the moonlight disappeared. Jamie turned towards the house and looked up past the grey misty shape of the upstairs veranda to the dark smudges that were the two towering chimneys pointing to the sky. Then he bent his knees slightly, took a jump and launched himself into the air. Safely in his arms, I held my breath as we sailed up the front wall of the house and over the roof, swerving deftly to miss one of the chimneys. The neighbours' houses grew smaller, then disappeared as we went higher. Quite quickly, we burst through the fog duvet and into the bright, moonlit air. Beyond the city, snow on the Southern Alps caught the moonlight and the ocean shone like a white tablecloth under a fluorescent light. Higher and higher we went.

Without moving, and all the time with his night-light glow, Jamie carried me further away from Earth. We went on until he pointed to a star that seemed to glow whiter and brighter than all the others. 'Alpha Centauri,' I said silently. 'One of the Pointers.' I knew this from having read Boy's encyclopaedia over his shoulder.

We flew by, then past, Beta Centauri until, before us, lay the Southern Cross. Glowing and beckoning, almost calling to me.

Jamie slowed and shifted his weight so that his torso angled further forward. He tucked me under one arm and flew on with his free arm stretching before him. We progressed like this until he was able to reach out and catch hold of the nearest star that was part of the glowing crown, the crown I had watched that night from the edge of the lake, and the same crown that was printed on my box from the toy shop. Jamie pulled the coronet of stars towards us and, as he did so, it reshaped itself, becoming small enough to sit comfortably above my ears when he placed it on my head.

Like a burst of lemonade from a shaken bottle, the promise of those stars surged through my body. I lowered my head and watched as thick golden fur rippled across my chest and arms like a breeze in a paddock of new wheat. The patches Boy's grandmother had made, and the coloured wool and cotton holding my ears in place, fell away. My legs, just visible beneath Jamie's arm, were firm and straight, lustrous and hairy. I was new again! I had been reborn! I looked as I did the day Jamie, and later Boy, opened the box from the toy shop.

Jamie's face was beaming. And reflected in his sparkling eyes I could see my own — two dazzling golden orbs sitting either side of a shiny black nose.

For the first time, Jamie, with his mouth closed and smiling, spoke.

'Now, the most important task of the evening,' he said. 'There is someone who must see you as you really are, your true self.'

He released his hold and I floated free for a moment before he gently, with a forefinger and thumb, took my paw. The Pointers turned as we passed, and followed our passage back to Earth, all the time pointing at the crown on my head as they had done for eons. As we approached the city, the last of the fog slipped off to the west to settle over the plains that sat at the feet of the mountains. The chimneys of the house on the hill loomed up clear and sharp in the night air and the smoke from the wood-burner wrapped us briefly in a warm grey blanket.

We landed lightly on the street in front of the house. Jamie led me under the arch in the hedge, through the garden all black and white in the moonlight, and across the porch to the front door. We passed through the door without opening it and moved along the hall, our legs motionless. When we reached Boy's room, Jamie let go of my paw and pushed me forward. I floated into the room.

Boy was asleep on his back. I turned to look at Jamie. He had gone. Boy moved, and I could see he was dreaming. I watched him as his breathing changed. To me, he was still the child who curled beside me in his bed. Something in his dream was disturbing him. Once, he would have allowed me to join him, but for many years now he had blocked me out. But surely in my glorious new form he would want to spend time with me once more?

I hovered beside his bed, and as I stared at his face with my two sparkling eyes, I quietly started to count backwards from ten. Ten, nine, eight, sev—

A barrier lifted like a gate at a car park, and I slipped into his dream.

The street was familiar even though it was night time. It was the street where the dairy stood in Invercargill fifty years ago. The finger-pointing sign pointed to the advertisements for creaming soda and banana splits. A bed of marigolds had replaced the petunias behind the thick concrete curb. Boy, now a man, stood with a threepence in his hand, unsure about going into the dairy to buy some chews. As he hesitated, the door swung open and a huge bulldog came lumbering out. The beast took its time, because it was held back by a lead in the hand of Boy's grandmother. She seemed younger and certainly in no need of a walking stick. On her arm she carried a basket. And sitting in that basket was me, a handsome new bear covered in golden fur with two sparkly glass eyes. A bright blue ribbon was tied in a bow under my chin. She allowed the beast to pull her out onto the street. Boy fell back and stood by the pointing finger. He watched as his mother and father came out of the shop, followed by his baby brother on the trike that Boy used to ride when he was in Invercargill on holiday.

On a radio, from somewhere inside the dairy, Uncle Clarrie's request session was playing 'The Teddy Bears' Picnic' for Sandy and Maurice of Venus Street.

If you go down to the woods today you're sure of a big surprise.

If you go down to the woods today you'd better go in disguise.

The grandmother, the boys' mum and dad, and BB started to tap their toes to the catchy tune. The beast strained on his lead. He was keen to get going. At the start of the second verse, they began to dance and sing.

For every bear that ever there was will gather there for certain because

Today's the day the teddy bears have their picnic.

Round and round Boy they danced as he crouched behind the pointing finger.

Six times they circled Boy before the beast broke away and led the dancers off down the street. Off and on the footpath he skipped on his short legs, into the gutter and out again. The others followed like a twisting snake. BB on his trike stayed on the footpath.

Boy came out from behind the finger and hurried to catch up. As the dancing snake passed houses of friends and neighbours, others joined in. Jimmy Cooke and his mother. Bubs Wood and her five kids; old Miss Frost; and last of all, from the little unpainted cottage with a dead Morris Minor lying on the overgrown lawn, Frankie Gibbs. Everyone was singing.

Every teddy bear who's been good is sure of a treat today,
There's lots of marvellous things to eat and wonderful games
to play.

The street lights lit the singing serpent as it danced past the houses with their little front gates you could step over, past the basilica, over the railway line and through the gap in the macrocarpa hedge into the Number Two Gardens.

Beneath the trees where nobody sees they'll hide and seek as
long as they please,
'Cause that's the way the teddy bears have their picnic.

The gravel path led the singing snake to the aviary where the birds sat quietly waiting. At the wire netting, the snake broke into pieces and became family and friends and neighbours again. The dancing stopped. And so did the singing. A goods train from Dunedin roared past on the other side of the hedge.

Boy, trying not to make too much noise, came along the edge of the crunchy path behind the small crowd, who were looking into the cage of birds. It was lit by a single light bulb, high up on a lamp-post. The kea was showing off as usual, and the peacock was spreading his tail, competing for attention. The other birds remained quiet and were watching the beast.

As Boy approached, the small group turned as one to

face him. His grandmother, still carrying me in her basket, came forward. She held the beast's lead. He sat down at her feet.

The Canary Island date palm behind the aviary waved its fronds in the air as if it to say it knew the answer to a question that someone had asked.

The grandmother picked me out of the basket and placed me in Boy's arms. 'I want to make a gift of this bear to you once more. You have another chance to take care of him.'

Boy looked down at me and smiled. My eyes sparkled, and I glowed all over like a pot of gold at the end of a rainbow.

The wind beneath the arms of the palm grew stronger. Boy's grandmother and the beast, his mum and dad, BB on the trike, Jimmy Cooke and his mother, Bubs Wood and her kids, and best friend Frankie Gibbs pulled their jackets and jerseys close as it grew colder. Leaves rose up as a cloud, and covered the people and the dog as they swirled around. Some stuck to the wire wall of the aviary. Then, just as quickly, the wind grew quiet. The leaves dropped back onto the paths and lawns of the Number Two Gardens.

When Boy looked up, he was alone. On his own, except for me.

30
THE GOLDEN YEARS

THE SHARP EDGES OF BOY'S DREAM slowly softened and dissolved. The aviary and the gardens slipped away until I was once more back in the rubbish bag, looking out of the gash with my button eye. It was still night time and the basement was dark and quiet except for the hum of the deep freeze. I was tingling with excitement. I had been shown my true worth by little Jamie, and had once more shared a dream and an adventure full of excitement and fear with Boy. It didn't matter what happened to me now. If I was to spend the rest of my days in a rubbish bag, I wouldn't mind. There was nothing more I could wish for.

Then the basement door opened. Boy came in. The deep freeze purred, expecting to be opened, the washing machine stood on stand-by, waiting to be filled with laundry, but Boy walked past both of them. He came right up to my bag, took it off the nail, tore it open and lifted me out. My left arm hung by a thread, my right hip was higher than my left, and the view of Boy's face was blurry through my button eye.

'Great!' he said. 'You are still here!'

Where did he think I would be? I wondered.

'I had a dream last night that has given me a great idea for a new book.'

And, just like the old days, he tucked me under his arm and took me upstairs. In his studio, he propped me up in the chair next to his and switched on the computer. He turned to me and beamed.

'I'm going to write the best book ever written. It's going to be exciting, scary, funny and heart-warming, and it's going to be about me when I was kid,' he said. 'And you are going to help!'

I smiled to myself.

'Now where will I start?'

With a slight frown, he looked deeply into my one glass eye. He could see himself reflected in there.

'I know — BB's birth! Can't remember much before that. That's when I got you — all wrapped up in a big brown paper parcel with lots of string.'

'But I came in a big box from Southern Cross Toys!' I shouted silently.

'Yeah, that's right,' he said. 'And I made a batman cape out of the brown paper to wear on my trike. It flew out behind me as I ran away to see the birds the next day.'

I sighed. He began tapping at the keyboard.

'Now I remember,' he continued. 'I chased that big bulldog at the dairy on the way home. Mamma thought I would be scared of him, but I wasn't.'

This wasn't going well. He was getting it all wrong. His memory was letting him down.

He turned once more from the computer and looked into my eye.

'BB was really rough with you, almost tore your ears off. Yanked off your arms too. Even chewed off one of your eyes! Gave you that stupid name. But I stuck up for you, protected you.'

I groaned.

'Yep, you would have ended up in the rubbish dump if I hadn't looked after you.'

Boy wrote on and on, stopping from time to time to stare into my eye. This seemed to give him inspiration, ideas for his next chapter.

'And wow, we had a terrific time in Kingston. I did some crazy things there, even when I was really little. I used to milk the cow on my own. Man, it was funny when the cow put its foot in a full bucket of milk. It was BB's fault, of course. He was pulling its tail.

'And on Guy Fawkes night I held two Catherine Wheels, one in each hand! I got a few burns, but I didn't care.

'And what's more, when I was only seven, I read a grown-ups' book all by myself. It was called *Burt Featherston and the Pirates*. Frankie Gibbs was dying to read it, too, but he couldn't. It was too hard.'

Occasionally he would ask, without turning his head, about names and places he couldn't remember.

'Who was the little kid who had a bright red jersey with swans around the waist?'

I would silently reply, 'Do you mean Rosie Garthwaite?'

He would pause for a while. 'Yeah, that's right, little

Maisie, Maisie Braithwaite!'

'Rosie,' I corrected. But he didn't hear me. He was already on to the next chapter about his sixth birthday party, and the huge sponge cake covered with whipped cream which he and Frankie Gibbs ate with their bare hands.

Sometimes his gaze would slide from my glass eye to the button eye where his reflection was dark and cloudy. His smile slipped from his face as memories he would rather have forgotten came into his head.

He shuddered at the thought of his wheelbarrow stuck on the railway line, unable to go forward or back, when the train was coming. And he went hot and cold remembering the bull that chased Frankie and him across Archie McCain's paddock. Memories of his fights with BB lurked in this eye too.

These excursions into dark places didn't last long. Boy was quick to shift his gaze from the button eye to the bright sparkly one, to remember again the fun and adventures he had had when he was a boy and when I was his best friend.

As he wrote, I thrilled once more at the excitement of his dare-devil rides with me in the back of his trike, and at our wild adventures in the wheelbarrow as he raced along the side of the railway tracks. Excitement and fear. We were doing it all over again. And, as in the days when both of us were young, we were doing it together.

At the end of each day, when Boy had finished his work, I remained in the chair beside his desk and looked out of the tall window in front of me, my glass eye scanning the night sky.

On clear nights the sky tingled with stars. Millions of stars, beyond counting. Some stars singled themselves out to be noticed. Orion dominated the north-western sky. The Scorpion sat in the brightest part of the Milky Way, and comets raced against the black ceiling with its sparkling lanterns almost too fast to be seen.

But it was the Pointers I looked for, Alpha and Beta Centauri, directing my gaze to the stars of the Southern Cross. And like the stars on the lid of the box from Southern Cross Toys, they stood out brighter than all the other stars in the sky.

Those four stars reminded of my beginnings — of the toy makers who made me and the children who loved me. Over the years they had been there to give me strength when I thought all was lost, a light of hope in the darkness. They reminded me that beneath my exterior of torn ears, mismatched eyes and patchy fur, I was still the same bear on the inside, not Teddy One-eye, nor Mrs Teddy, but Mr Edward K. Bear, a toy to be loved.

And when little Jamie placed the crown of stars on my head, he showed me I was a special bear — a bear with a past as well as one with a future.

ACKNOWLEDGEMENTS

Lyrics to 'Teddy Bears' Picnic', Henry Hall.

Ruth Fielding and the Gypsies or The Missing Pearl Necklace, Alice B. Emerson, Cupples & Leon Company, 1915.

Note: The word 'lisle' (lisle stockings) is pronounced as 'lyall.'

Gavin Bishop is a highly acclaimed children's book author and illustrator. Born in Invercargill, he spent his childhood in the remote railway settlement of Kingston on the shores of Lake Wakatipu. Studying under Russell Clark and Rudi Gopas, Gavin graduated from the Canterbury University School of Fine Arts with an honours degree in painting. He taught art at Linwood High School (now Linwood College) and at Christ's College in Christchurch.

He won the Margaret Mahy Medal in 2000, and has also won numerous other fellowships and national book awards. His book *The House that Jack Built* won the Book of the Year and Best Picture Book at the NZ Post Children's Book Awards 2000. *Weaving Earth and Sky* won the non-fiction section and the Book of the Year Award of the NZ Post Children's Book Awards 2003, and was shortlisted for the LIANZA Elsie Lock Medal in 2003. He has won the LIANZA Russell Clark Medal for Illustration four times. Among his successful partnerships has been that with writer Joy Cowley, with whom he won the Best in Junior Fiction and Book of the Year at the 2008 NZ Post Children's Book Awards for *Snake and Lizard*.

The Storylines Gavin Bishop Award for Picture Book Illustration was established in 2009 to encourage emergent illustrators and to acknowledge Gavin's contribution to the writing and illustrating of children's picture books. In 2013 he was made an Officer of the New Zealand Order of Merit, and President of Honour of the NZ Society of Authors, and he was the recipient of the 2013 Arts Foundation Mallinson Rendel Illustrator's Award. Gavin's artwork has featured in exhibitions internationally, including Japan and Czechoslovakia. He has written and designed two ballets for the Royal New Zealand Ballet Company: *Terrible Tom* and *Te Maia and the Sea Devil*. In 2003, during the Ursula Bethell Residency, he wrote and illustrated *Giant Jimmy Jones*, the world's first three-dimensional animated picture book for HITLab at the University of Canterbury.

See more about Gavin at www.gavinbishop.com.

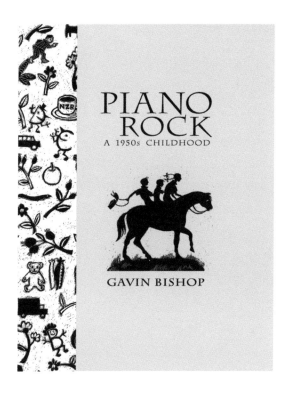

PIANO ROCK

This charming award-winning book is a memoir of Gavin Bishop's idyllic childhood days, growing up in Kingston beside gorgeous Lake Wakatipu. It's a gentle tale of a boyhood spent haring around outside, building huts, eating girdle scones, catching eels, watching the train, eating roast mutton, going to school on a horse, arguing with his best mate, eating Marmite sandwiches, Guy Fawkes Day — and lots more eating.

For more information about our titles please visit
www.randomhouse.co.nz